Ozhoma

OZHOMA

By
Trygve Jorgensen

RESOURCE *Publications* • Eugene, Oregon

OZHOMA

Resource Publications
An Imprint of Wipf and Stock Publishers
199 W. 8th Ave., Suite 3
Eugene, OR 97401

www.wipfandstock.com

PAPERBACK ISBN: 978-1-6667-0328-3
HARDCOVER ISBN: 978-1-6667-0329-0
EBOOK ISBN: 978-1-6667-0330-6

06/29/21

Prologue

Her beautiful little eyes stare at Nuyaka Creek while it trickles away into the Deep Fork. Nuyaka Creek, in its beneficence, gives itself into the watershed that drains into the city of Okmulgee in Indian Territory. Okmulgee is where learned lawyers will soon litigate her worth before their palaces dedicated more to what Creeks call *tokvnawa* than the immigrant's blind goddess. The Deep Fork has little streams that, tendril-like, truncate from it, open veins nourishing the earth, trees, frogs, bugs, life. In her line of sight there is a rag on the bank of the rivulet, its blackened cotton is strewn just below her. The cloth is not covered with any unguent, yet from it streams an oleograph. The pattern from it is dreamlike; it makes the water surface look strange, like a distorted rainbow, and it floats away. In her eight years she saw too much sadness and then the final terror came like a shape-shifter, in the dark, with no mercy. Her cousin is still as well and they are cruelly free from their shared terror. Their little bodies will soon join the animals who become soil. Animals whose decaying form under pressure by Mother Earth makes kerogen, a product that will be named *kulgee neeha* by her people, petroleum by avaricious wildcats. Her life liquids will become distorted by death in time but not soon enough for the gaunt wallets of those who worship mammon by boiling the black liquid of decay; boiling their sin. Idolaters whose gold-painted statue stands much like Caligula's, a desecration in the holy of holies, a totem to their God of wealth in Tulsa stands.

The little girl is Ullie Eagle and she will not hear the cow horn blow at Tuskeegee church a little ways from her. She will not smell *sofke* or hear Muscogee sorrow. She will never see the tears flow from the Lighthorseman's eyes as he cuts the rope to give her freedom the next day.

Tokvnawa=Money
Unguent= Ointment
Oleograph=pattern of oil on water
Mammon=Wealth that is worshipped

The Muscogee called the Lighthorsemen *Este Wanayv*; it means "ties men up," not children. The rope he cut was not his, and it looks worn from being thrown around a cathead. She never heard him tenderly sing to her an ancient ceremonial song, one nuanced by the grief it found on the long walk from Alabama. She will never know that beneath his tin badge, she broke his heart.

CHAPTER 1

Eben boards the train to begin his long trip home. Ebenezer Kowee Baker is a former tribal rail inspector for the Choctaw Treasury, a displaced lawman with no avenue to justice. He rides now in metal probably forged or at least purchased with McAlester coal. He had loved being an inspector because he stood like a cellulose warrior fighting against Gould-sized greed. Forty years have passed since that time. How many presidents knew or were former rail attorneys? He can't tell you, but he can tell you that where avarice is there is someone being stolen from and usually they are brown. *Kowee* in Choctaw means "mountain lion." Interestingly he is remarkably built like a mountain lion, with a large chest and athletic arms, yet he is horizontally challenged at five feet five inches. A pensive face belies the humor in his heart. His face seems wrinkled with worry or doubt. You could say he looks like any Choctaw man of his generation, but then end up with some reference to Catlin pictures of Moshulatubbee or stickball payers with horsehair tails. His face is generally oval with cheekbones that some might mistake for those of a chipmunk; cordial, yet serious. Oh be serious, all Indians look the same—either Adam Beach or Wes Studi, take your mental pic.

Trains always make Eben think of home, which is near a town named "Metal Road" where a depot stands under a sign baptized in his language "Talihina." He watches other people's houses. Other people's farms and some tall trees probably saplings at the time of removal blur past the vibrating window. Nostalgia is not lost on Choctaw; they love reliving the past like everyone. "They've come to steal everything again," is what his aunties used to say. Eben could picture them stirring *tanche labuna* outside their church camphouse. In the shade of pine, hickory, and blackjack trees the old women would talk about men, kids, and occasionally politics. Mostly they hoped that God would

Avarice=extreme Greed
Tanche labuna=Hominy Dish
Cathead=Drilling Rig motor flywheel used like a pulley.

make all things right. He remembered listening to their distress reading the *Choctaw Vindicator*'s announcement that Congress had adopted the Oklahoma Enabling Act. This crushed the salvation scheme of the state of Sequoyah, their last hope. He remembers this conversation so vividly from thirty years earlier in 1906, because all memory for Choctaw men is tied to their stomach and pig meat with hominy is Indun soul food.

The tracks stretch out in front as it curves among pine forests that look uncannily like Talihina. Testimony before the House of Representatives on why the five tribes should be allowed to reorganize under the Oklahoma Indian Welfare Act (OIWA) was exhausting. Listening to tribes described as socialistic enclaves by Oklahoma Representative Disney made his head sweat. *What the hell is socialism?* Congressional Oklahomans were trying to paint the President as a commie and his Indian programs were the tip of the sickle back in Oklahoma. Eventually after the OIWA is adopted the Choctaw Agency will move to Talihina, and soon the WPA will start building the New-Deal rock hospital nestled in stately pines. Talihina, and the path of steel he is on now, stirs embers of all the politics that metal brings, especially Choctaw politics. The steady rocking is perfect for reflection. Thoughts have captured his energy and now he twists a strategy of how to help his family map a survival plan in this new era. He, like warriors of old, who braided squirrel hide into bowstring, must attempt to braid the new politics. He is bound for Tulsa out of Washington, DC. in the early morning, a trip back that ambassadors from his tribe had made numerous times, and which he has made twice himself.

His iron road to DC gained impetus from his need to help families he knew personally; everything is personal in politics. He was an advocate without purse, an evangelist without calling. Lost causes always shape our politics and Dicey Nuwa had shaped Eben's.

Hoshe Dicey Nuwa, was her name. Hoshe means "bird" and Nuwa means "to walk" in Chahta. She lived at the end of a wagon rut in a one-room shack with her daughter, son, and niece. Dicey had suffered burns across her back during a brush fire near the original location of the house and nearly died, the women of the church nursing her through torment with prayers and tears. The fire had molded her fragile body and made her lean to one side, with skin pulled taut from scarring. Moving forward she had to summon an enormous will to fight her body's predilection to turn to the right in meaningless circles, always overstepping to correct her course.

She was full of God and she is the story that makes you question why she never curses heaven.

You could see glimpses of how lovely she had been before the scars. If you had met her when she was younger, you would have thought she was the reason the Choctaw conceived of the Sun Goddess, full of brightness that exudes from kind humor. Long dark hair, pulled up into a bun, soft smiles hidden with lips pulled tight against her teeth. Now the brightness shines through her eyes while the skin is discolored from fire, as if her inner sunlight has burned through the shroud of flesh.

The shack she lives in now is barely ten yards from where the original house had been erected after her nuptials at Big Lick Church. By modern standards her shack would have been appraised as little more than a big chicken coop, but poor folks have poor ways and every nest has its own comfort. It was customary for the relatives of the newlyweds to gather and build the cabin during the weekend as a blessing. Uncles and cousins using bandsaws to cut down pine trees for the logs, notching with axes. Some relatives would make shingles while the others erected the structure. The mothers of the married children would handle the logistics and labor management, providing direction, correction, and food to those wise enough to request by supplication. Dicey's honeymoon was short-lived though, even before her skin faced flames.

Within two years of being married she delivered her son after previously suffering a miscarriage. Then her husband, a man without the sense God gave a goose, caught pneumonia working in the cold rain without his hat, wet damp chilling his core to the bone. No amount of salve would help him catch his breath. He lost so much weight that he resembled a scarecrow with wooden arms protruding from withered flesh. Winter seemed to rob him of the will to live, stealing first his strength and then his color. Eben remembered Dicey wailing during the funeral, collapsing at the gravesite, and that was the first time she made him cry. Her husband skidded logs and the loss of his labor made impoverishment even more torturous.

Then the following summer was dry and she was making lye in the yard. Lye is used to prepare hominy since it will break down dent corn's hard shell. Then the remainder could be combined with rendered hog fat for soap. She had been scooping the ashes to pour into the boiling water when a cinder from under her kettle blew into brush that exploded into fury. The flames would erupt too near her home in her garden of corn, now dried like harvest sentinels. For some reason she thought she could fight it. Why tragedy haunts some is hard to know, but suffering did not refrain from visiting her.

A year later, in 1909, her sister and her brother-in-law died in a tragic, mysterious house fire, leaving their daughter orphaned. Little orphan Annie had no Daddy Warbucks and was found sleeping in the chicken coop, baby chicks cheeping around her. Dicey received notice in the mail three days later of her sister's circumstance. She had the pastor take her by buckboard to Wilburton where her niece was. The next week the girl was living with Dicey. Dicey's new daughter was named Annie, named for a grandmother.

"Speak up for those who cannot speak for themselves," that's what Proverbs says. His testimony before Congress was on behalf of Dicey, he thought, but mostly for all the Annies he knew.

"*Halito,* Eben," Dicey said that Christmas morning in 1910. Eben had been asked to exhort about the Christ child and was traveling from camphouse to camphouse to greet and eat.

"*Halito,* Dicey," Eben replied cheerfully.

"I been meaning to speak to you," she said, smiling while looking out the screen door past Eben, not rudely, but in a polite, formal way, to signal her humility that was already clothed in natural shyness.

"Sorry If I spoke too long." Eben's joke received a hidden giggle from behind her hand.

"No, your momma told me that you knew how to read white man's way and that you could tell me what this letter means." She produced a multi-folded letter out of her hymnal.

Eben leaned against the door frame, listening to the muffled conversations around him, glancing at old men's cheeks, full like chipmunks, chewing biscuit with fried hog meat. He read the letter silently, deliberately sounding out the words to begin the mental translation; his vocabulary had begun to purposefully atrophy since his welcome exile to Nashoba.

"Well, Dicey, this paper says that Annie's guardian has been putting her royalty payments in an account. Did you know that she had a guardian?"

"What's that word mean?" Dicey looked perplexed.

"Well that means that Annie has an attorney who is in charge of her money." While speaking, he explored Dicey's features to see if she comprehended.

"What money?" Dicey asked, even more astounded.

"Did your sister have some?" Eben asked dumb questions with the best of them.

"No!"

"Well this money is coming from somewhere. Has Annie been getting any money?"

"No."

"Well, see, royalties are usually from coal around here and I guess that they may be mining on her daddy's land, you think? At any rate, it says on the paper that attorney costs, preparation costs, filing costs, and other costs have been charged to her account. Did you pay for any of those costs?" Eben reread the letter while Dicey shook her head, unaware of anything he was speaking of.

"When I picked up Annie she was at some white man's house. This black woman met us at the door and took me immediately to Annie who was asleep on a pallet in this room. When Annie woke up she thought I was her momma at first and cried as she jumped in my arms. Then she realized it was me, I guess her eyes were too puffy from crying. Anyways, after a while a white man came from in town and introduced himself to me, and Pastor Frazier was there of course. He showed us some papers to sign. I didn't understand his words, and the pastor thought he was telling me that I had to sign for Annie."

"Do you have a copy of what you signed, Dicey?" Eben asked, growing concerned.

"No, he said he would take care of them for me."

"After New Year's, if you like, I will travel to Wilburton to speak to this white man. Was his name Daniel Smith? The name here on this letter?" Eben pointed to the name on the stationary.

"I think that's right." Dicey seemed relieved to hear this. "I thought they was going to take Annie away and I took that letter and folded it in my hands and prayed and prayed and prayed that God would please take care of us. I haven't seen any letter like this before and I was for sure that it meant something bad, and then God gave me a dream and don't you know in that dream I was talking to you. It must be a good sign."

Dicey smiled easily and reached out with her scarred hand to touch Eben's arm.

CHAPTER 2

The community of Edna sits not far from the tribal town of Tuskegee and on the banks of Nuyaka Creek. Tuskegee is the name of one of the original forty-four confederated tribes called Tribal Towns. Now Tuskegee Baptist Church sits under large oaks, a covered porch is used in the summer with two-by-four pews needing a second coat of paint.

A simple lesson. England divided its realm by a feudal hierarchal structure. The King ruled the Dukes, who ruled the Counts, who ruled the Knights, who ruled the Peasants. Wealthy lords, be they Kings, Dukes, or Counts, therefore had castles. Very patriarchal and obsessed with fees. Call feuds over fees among the elite a vernacular word "war" and the jockeying for land and control makes sense. Eventually the monarchs that ruled England would go even farther by making the hierarchy an extension of heaven: the Father, his son Jesus, and his appointed adopted son the King, whose seed determined the line of succession. In Rome there was an attempt to place the Pope on a level higher than kings, but that's a whole other lesson.

Tribal Towns are sub-kingdoms. More appropriately queendoms. The *Micco* (Leader) is only so because his mother is the Clan Mother. His oldest sister's oldest son becomes the next prince; matrilineal descent based on the ovum. Other relatives hold status based on function. In times of war, the lead warrior becomes the War Leader. Thus the Micco-Leader represents the White Town aspect of the queendom; diplomacy and consensus. The War Leader represents the Red Town aspect of the queendom; defense and alliance. The Micco-Leader reveals his leadership through a speaker. Think of the speaker like a Secretary of State. The Medicine Man holds the fourth estate as the spiritual advisor. In essence four leaders for the four winds. The Muscogee confederacy in Indian Territory developed a council where forty-four leaders from the queendoms called Town Kings presided over a body like the senate, and forty-four leaders called Town Warriors would preside over a body like the House of Representatives, with additional representation based on census.

Nuyaka is a member of this ancient council. Nuyaka is famous because when the first treaty of 1786 was signed it was done so at the original capitol of the United States in New York City. Some of the Muscogee delegates were so impressed with the city they renamed their queendom after the treaty site; New York in the east and Nuyaka in Indian Territory. New York bankers will become feudal financiers in the exploration of oil in Nuyaka. Nuyaka Mission was established by the Presbyterians.

Eagles in the English language have no gender designation and thus are equal. The male is not called the rooster, nor is the female called the hen. Yet Ullie is named for her father and not her mother. European patrilineal society imposing on Muscogee matrilineal families. When she was an egg, whose egg was she? Ullie Eagle is listed as eight years of age, female, full-blood Creek, roll #4338, on Dawes Allotment Card 1357. Sealie, age 90, is also listed on the same card. Toochie and David are not.

In Oklahoma, the battlefield moved from feudal investiture to corporate strategy. The case to decide whose egg or sperm would prevail became the field of battle. The file from Muskogee read:

Department of the Interior, United States Indian Superintendent, and June 23, 1913. In the matter of the protest against the approval of oil and gas mining lease #24200, Nellie Fish et al, as sole heirs of Ullie Eagle, deceased. Protest of Hill Oil & Gas Company, represented by P. E. McGee, Attorney at law, of Tulsa, Oklahoma. Lessee, Jos. A. Chapman, represented by H. H. Rogers, of Tulsa and Holdenville, Oklahoma. Witnesses: Katie Bear, David Harry, Marsie Harry, Susie Tiger now Malone, J. E. Thrift, Legus Brown, US Indian Interpreter.

David Harry, called as a witness, being duly sworn, by L. W. Jones, Notary Public, for Creek County, Oklahoma, testified as follows:

EXAMINATION BY P. E. MCGEE. (Hill Oil & Gas)

Q. You may state your name? (Hill O&G $26,000,000 at stake)

A. (Muscogee trapped by Dead Indian Act, through interpreter, here and throughout) David Harry.

Q. Where do you live? (Hill O&G $26,000,000 at stake)

A. (BY INTERPRETER) Nine miles west of Beggs.

Q. How long have you lived there? (Hill O&G $26,000,000 at stake)

A. (BY INTERPRETER) I am living there at this time.

Q. How old are you? (Hill O&G $26,000,000 at stake)

A. (BY INTERPRETER) Sixty years old.

Q. Are you a citizen of the Creek Nation? (Hill O&G $26,000,000 at stake)

A. (BY INTERPRETER) Yes, sir.

Q. Did you know Ullie Eagle in her lifetime? (Hill O&G $26,000,000 at stake)

A. (BY INTERPRETER) Yes, sir.

Q. Where did she live? (Hill O&G $26,000,000 at stake)

A. (BY INTERPRETER) Used to live about five or six miles west of Edna.

Q. How far from where you live? (Hill O&G $26,000,000 at stake)

A. (BY INTERPRETER) Four or five miles.

Q. Do you know when Ullie Eagle died? (Hill O&G $26,000,000 at stake)

A. (BY INTERPRETER) I know she died, I can't tell just what year.

Q. Do you know what caused her death? (Hill O&G $26,000,000 at stake)

A. (BY INTERPRETER) I have heard of it.

Q. Do you know about when she died? (Hill O&G $26,000,000 at stake)

A. (BY INTERPRETER) I could not state what year it was, I know she died; it looks to me as if it was somewhere in the spring, in May or June, I could not state exactly what month it was.

If it is late June then the tribal town queendoms are full of energy with Green Corn Festivals on the horizon. The event calls families by the hundreds into the woods to dance around ceremonial fires whose embers were carried on the trail of tears to reestablish them in the new homeland. Green Corn festivals mean that the traditional games of stickball have begun and the ceremonial stomp dances run long into the night across the land of the Muscogee people. July welcomes the new year for the celebrants. Europeans celebrate the winter solstice and the Muscogee the summer solstice; polar opposite in orientation. Europeans celebrate the middle of the starving time and Muscogee celebrate the middle of the time to feast. Europeans celebrate the male who must bring in the food hunted and killed and the Muscogee celebrate the female because Mother Earth brings her cornucopia of gifts.

Q. Is there anything that happened along about that time, you can think of, that would fix the date? (Hill O&G $26,000,000 at stake)

A. (BY INTERPRETER) Well, yes. It happened at that time, I believe, the Creek people had a scrimmage with each other; a little stirring up, something like that.

Stickball is a game that the French called lacrosse. It is played at ceremonial grounds to celebrate the game which was given from the creator. The game was given to end senseless bloodshed that occurred during disputes of territory or clan laws. The queendoms were shown a way to settle the disputes on a ball field. Think of it as lacrosse, played with body-checking allowed. The queendom whose players prevail also win the dispute; the Muscogee call such events *daebothetha*. A scrimmage therefore would be more game than pain. The friendly form of the game is usually East vs. West and the Medicine Men sing songs to encourage their sides, while they keep record with little sticks stuck in the ground for each score.

Q. Do you know who Ullie's mother was? (Hill O&G $26,000,000 at stake)

A. (BY INTERPRETER) Yes.

Q. Who was it? (Hill O&G $26,000,000 at stake)

A. (BY INTERPRETER) Toochie.

Q. Is Toochie dead or alive? (Hill O&G $26,000,000 at stake)

A. (BY INTERPRETER) Dead.

Q. When did she die? (Hill O&G $26,000,000 at stake)

A. (BY INTERPRETER) I could not tell just what year she died.

Q. She die before or after Ullie? (Hill O&G $26,000,000 at stake)

A. (BY INTERPRETER) I think before.

Q. Who was Ullie's father? (Hill O&G $26,000,000 at stake)

A. (BY INTERPRETER) Dave Eagle.

Q. Is he dead or alive? (Hill O&G $26,000,000 at stake)

A. (BY INTERPRETER) Dead.

Q. When did he die? (Hill O&G $26,000,000 at stake)

A. (BY INTERPRETER) I could not remember what year it was; been quite a little while.

Q. Died before or after Toochie? (Hill O&G $26,000,000 at stake)

A. (BY INTERPRETER) Yes, sir.

Q. Before Ullie? (Hill O&G $26,000,000 at stake)

A. (BY INTERPRETER) Yes, sir.

Q. Who was Toochie's mother? (Hill O&G $26,000,000 at stake)

A. (BY INTERPRETER) Toochie's mother was ——

Q. Mr. Rogers (McMan Oil & Gas, i.e., Chapman-McFarlin): I object to witness's memory being refreshed.

A. (BY INTERPRETER) I know it already.

Q. Did you know her? (Hill O&G $26,000,000 at stake)

A. (BY INTERPRETER) Yes, sir.

Q. Where did she live? (Hill O&G $26,000,000 at stake)

A. (BY INTERPRETER) Lived close to Edna, all used to live close together.

Edna, where Tuskegee Church is located is now within Creek County for Oklahoma. Originally Edna would have been in the Okmulgee District for the confederacy. Had the state of Sequoyah been admitted it is likely that Edna would have been in Tulladega County. As the seal of Oklahoma legislation states, "the peaceful conquest of the Anglo Saxon," and thus no Tulladega, and it is named Creek County. Renaming is always the least painful experience of peaceful conquest.

Q. Did you know when she died? (Hill O&G $26,000,000 at stake)

A. (BY INTERPRETER) No, sir, I could not state. I know she is dead but never have any recollection; just hear when she is dead, that settles it.

Q. Do you know whether she died before Toochie? (Hill O&G $26,000,000 at stake)

A. (BY INTERPRETER) Yes, sir.

Q. Did Toochie's mother die before Toochie died? (Hill O&G $26,000,000 at stake)

A. (BY INTERPRETER) Yes, sir, I think it was?

Q. Do you know who she lived with? (Hill O&G $26,000,000 at stake)

A. (BY INTERPRETER) Toochie's mother?

Q. Yes, sir. (Hill O&G $26,000,000 at stake)

A. (BY INTERPRETER) She used to live with her sister?

Q. Who was her sister? (Hill O&G $26,000,000 at stake)

A. (BY INTERPRETER) Katie Bear.

Q. Was she living with Katie Bear at the time she died? (Hill O&G $26,000,000 at stake)

A. (BY INTERPRETER) I don't know whether she was or not.

Q. Do you know who Toochie's father was? (Hill O&G $26,000,000 at stake)

A. (BY INTERPRETER) No, sir.

Q. Did you know Toochie's father? (Hill O&G $26,000,000 at stake)

A. (BY INTERPRETER) Toochie's father, I might make a mistake, when I go to think it over, San-ta-le-fixico, I may be a little mistaken but it was a man by that name any way.

Q. Do you know whether it was the father? (Hill O&G $26,000,000 at stake)

A. (BY INTERPRETER) No answer.

Q. Do you know whether he was the father or husband of Toochie? (Hill O&G $26,000,000 at stake)

A. (BY INTERPRETER) I think it was his husband.

Q. Who was Ullie Eagle living with at the time she died? (Hill O&G $26,000,000 at stake)

A. (BY INTERPRETER) She was living with Katie Bear.

Q. From the time she was a baby she lived with Katie Bear? (Hill O&G $26,000,000 at stake)

A. (BY INTERPRETER) Yes, sir.

Q. Who supported her, Ullie Eagle? (Hill O&G $26,000,000 at stake)

Q. Mr. Rogers (McMan Oil & Gas, i.e., Chapman-McFarlin): I object to that as being incompetent, irrelevant, and immaterial; it is only a question of heirship. I don't think it would matter.

Q. Mr. McGee, I withdraw the question. Do you know who David Eagle's father was? (Hill O&G $26,000,000 at stake)

A. (BY INTERPRETER) Yes, sir.

Q. Who was his father? (Hill O&G $26,000,000 at stake)

A. (BY INTERPRETER) Man by the name of Hathan Harjo.

Q. Did Ullie Eagle have any brothers or sisters? (Hill O&G $26,000,000 at stake)

A. (BY INTERPRETER) No, sir, not any I know of.

Q. Would you likely have known if she did? (Hill O&G $26,000,000 at stake)

Q. Mr. Rogers (McMan Oil & Gas, i.e., Chapman-McFarlin): I believe that would be calling for a conclusion.

A. (BY INTERPRETER) She did not have any sisters at all.

Q. Did Toochie Eagle and David Eagle live together up to the time of David's death? (Hill O&G $26,000,000 at stake)

A. (BY INTERPRETER) Yes, sir.

Q. Was David Eagle ever married to anybody else? (Hill O&G $26,000,000 at stake)

A. (BY INTERPRETER) No, sir.

Q. Do you know whether Toochie ever married anybody else? (Hill O&G $26,000,000 at stake)

A. (BY INTERPRETER) No, sir.

CROSS EXAMINATION BY MR. ROGERS: (McMan Oil & Gas, i.e., Chapman-McFarlin)

H. H. Rogers was an attorney in Wewoka before he joined James Chapman and Robert McFarlin. Their company based in the notorious town of Holdenville was known as McMan Oil. H. H. Rogers, or rather Henry, would become the VP of Union National Bank in Tulsa and eventually be elected to the Oklahoma legislature as a Republican. It was Rogers who was assigned the task of purchasing land for McMan Oil. Angie Debo recorded in her book *And the Waters Still Run*, that land deeds in Holdenville were more likely to be forged than legitimate during this time.

Q. You say that Ullie didn't have any brothers and sisters? (McMan O&G 26,000,000 at stake)

A. (BY INTERPRETER) Who was that?

Q. Ullie? (McMan O&G 26,000,000 at stake)

A. (BY INTERPRETER) No, sir.

Q. How do you know? (McMan O&G 26,000,000 at stake)

A. (BY INTERPRETER) I supposed she was not married.

Q. Was you acquainted with David Eagle? (McMan O&G 26,000,000 at stake)

A. (BY INTERPRETER) Yes, sir.

Q. You saw David every other day? (McMan O&G 26,000,000 at stake)

A. (BY INTERPRETER) Well until he died.

Q. Most every other day? (McMan O&G 26,000,000 at stake)

A. (BY INTERPRETER) Saw him at ball playing going on.

Q. He never was away from that community? (McMan O&G 26,000,000 at stake)

A. (BY INTERPRETER) Yes, sir.

Q. Then you didn't see him every other day? (McMan O&G 26,000,000 at stake)

A. (BY INTERPRETER) No, sir. Sometimes four or five days apart.

Q. You didn't know how often you saw him? (McMan O&G 26,000,000 at stake)

A. (BY INTERPRETER) Every other day or so, every Saturday at the ball playing some times.

Q. You thought you saw him often? (McMan O&G 26,000,000 at stake)

A. (BY INTERPRETER) No, sir.

Q. Did you see Toochie all the time? (McMan O&G 26,000,000 at stake)

A. (BY INTERPRETER) Well, not all the time.

Q. You don't know whether she had any other children or not? (McMan O&G 26,000,000 at stake)

A. (BY INTERPRETER) I saw them just once in a while.

Q. How often did you see Toochie? (McMan O&G 26,000,000 at stake)

A. (BY INTERPRETER) About sometimes.

Q. I will ask you if Toochie had any other husband. (McMan O&G 26,000,000 at stake)

A. (BY INTERPRETER) I don't know.

Q. You say you don't know? (McMan O&G 26,000,000 at stake)

A. (BY INTERPRETER) No.

Q. You don't know whether she might have married somebody else and she might have some other children? (McMan O&G 26,000,000 at stake)

A. (BY INTERPRETER) I don't know.

Q. You don't know whether she was married or not? (McMan O&G 26,000,000 at stake)

A. (BY INTERPRETER) She . . .

Q. David Eagle have any sisters? (McMan O&G 26,000,000 at stake)

A. (BY INTERPRETER) Yes, sir.

Q. What was their names? (McMan O&G 26,000,000 at stake)

A. (BY INTERPRETER) Winney Tiger.

Q. Winney Tiger? (McMan O&G 26,000,000 at stake)

A. (BY INTERPRETER) Yes, sir.

Q. Live close to Okmulgee? (McMan O&G 26,000,000 at stake)

Mr. McGee: I object to refreshing the witness's memory.

Mr. Rogers (McMan Oil & Gas, i.e., Chapman-McFarlin): I withdraw the question.

Q. Where did this sister, Winney Tiger, live? (McMan O&G 26,000,000 at stake)

A. (BY INTERPRETER) Lived west of Edna. She married to a man by the name of Pufney Tiger, and that is David Eagle's sister; Pufney's daughter, that is David Eagle's sister.

Q. Is this Winney Tiger young or old lady? (McMan O&G 26,000,000 at stake)

A. (BY INTERPRETER) She was old lady.

Q. You say old woman? (McMan O&G 26,000,000 at stake)

A. (BY INTERPRETER) Yes, sir.

Q. How old is that woman that lived at Okmulgee? (McMan O&G 26,000,000 at stake)

A. (BY INTERPRETER) I know it was old Winney Tiger that died west of Beggs, that was long ago.

Q. Do you know that woman? (McMan O&G 26,000,000 at stake)

A. (BY INTERPRETER) Yes, sir.

Q. Old woman? (McMan O&G 26,000,000 at stake)

A. (BY INTERPRETER) Old woman, about seventy or eighty years old. (McMan O&G 26,000,000 at stake)

Q. You know her children? (McMan O&G 26,000,000 at stake)

A. (BY INTERPRETER) Which one, down at Okmulgee? (McMan O&G 26,000,000 at stake)

Q. Southwest of Beggs. (McMan O&G 26,000,000 at stake)

A. (BY INTERPRETER) That is all I know, there is two Winney Tigers, both dead.

Q. Either one leave any children? (McMan O&G 26,000,000 at stake)

A. (BY INTERPRETER) No, sir.

Q. Do you know whether they did or not? (McMan O&G 26,000,000 at stake)

A. (BY INTERPRETER) There was two Winney Tigers.

Q. Either one of them have children? (McMan O&G 26,000,000 at stake)

A. (BY INTERPRETER) Both had children, all dead.

Q. Which of these Winney Tigers that you testified about is dead now? (McMan O&G 26,000,000 at stake)

A. (BY INTERPRETER) I didn't say that, it might have had children afterwards.

Q. Which Winey might have had children afterwards? (McMan O&G 26,000,000 at stake)

A. (BY INTERPRETER) I don't know, I used to see them.

Q. What is the name of any living children of either one of the Winney about which you testified? (McMan O&G 26,000,000 at stake)

A. (BY INTERPRETER) I don't know.

Q. Did you know Susie Tiger? (McMan O&G 26,000,000 at stake)

A. (BY INTERPRETER) No, sir.

Q. I will ask you now if Susie Tiger is a daughter of Winney Tiger. (McMan O&G 26,000,000 at stake)

A. (BY INTERPRETER) I don't know.

Q. Do you know Timmie Jessie? (McMan O&G 26,000,000 at stake)

A. (BY INTERPRETER) Yes, sir.

Q. What kin to Toochie? (McMan O&G 26,000,000 at stake)

A. (BY INTERPRETER) I don't know.

Q. Do you know Nellie Fish? (McMan O&G 26,000,000 at stake)

A. (BY INTERPRETER) No, sir.

RE-EXAMINATION BY MR. MCGEE.

P. E. McGee (Hill Oil & Gas) was the Vice President of Hill Oil & Gas. William Carnill is listed as President. Hill Oil & Gas is noted in the January 1916 Fuel Oil Journal as selling their Cushing interest to Cosden Oil & Gas for $12,000,000.

Q. Do you remember the name of Toochie's mother? (Hill O&G $26,000,000 at stake)

A. (BY INTERPRETER) I can't remember.

Q. Do you remember the name of Katie Bear's sister? (Hill O&G $26,000,000 at stake)

A. (BY INTERPRETER) . . .

Q. To refresh your memory, was it Picimnie? (Hill O&G $26,000,000 at stake)

Mr. Rogers (McMan Oil & Gas, i.e., Chapman-McFarlin): Object to question and answer.

Q. Was it Secehuy? (Hill O&G $26,000,000 at stake)

A. (BY INTERPRETER) Secehuy was Katie Bear's sister.

EXAMINATION BY MR. WALKUP

Mr. Frank H. Walkup is identified as the Chief Clerk for the Bureau of Indian Affairs Muskogee Office. The tribe is spelled Muscogee but the city is named Muskogee. In hearings before the Committee on Investigation of the Indian Service in the House of Representatives we learn that the original office of the Commissioner to the Five Civilized Tribes consisted of a cashier's division, land office, unalloted lands, tribal divisions and mailing division. Under the BIA Superintendent's office Mr. Walkup lists the new divisions as cashiers division, mailing division, lease division, royalty division, restrictions, sales, payments and field division. Mr. Walkup earned a salary of $1,600 per year. Legus Brown, the interpreter, earned $30 per month.

Q. Was Secehuy married to the father of Toochie? (BIA)

A. (BY INTERPRETER) I don't know whether she was or not.

Q. Did they live together? (BIA)

A. (BY INTERPRETER) I don't know.

Q. You don't know whether they lived together as man and wife or not. (BIA)

A. (BY INTERPRETER) No, sir.

Q. Do you know if the husband of Secehuy left any relatives, either brothers or sisters? (BIA)

A. (BY INTERPRETER) No, sir.

Q. Secehuy have a husband? (BIA)

A. (BY INTERPRETER) No, sir, I don't know.

Q. You mean Secehuy husband? (BIA)

A. (BY INTERPRETER) No, sir.

Q. What was his name? (BIA)

A. (BY INTERPRETER) Santale Fixseko.

MR. ROGERS (McMan Oil & Gas, i.e., Chapman-McFarlin)

Q. I thought you said some Harjo? He said just before that some Harjo.

A. (BY INTERPRETER) I got mixed up in the name.

Q. You're kind of mixed up in the whole business? (McMan Oil & Gas, i.e., Chapman – McFarlin)

A. (BY INTERPRETER) No, sir.

CHAPTER 3

Eben borrows the pastor's buggy for the trip to Wilburton. He arrives at Dicey's house and she is two hours ready with a napkin in her hand to wipe sweat. Eben smiles broadly at little Annie. Her grin masks her toothless face. Her smile dims the sun. Annie is at that age where her knobby knees look like plums stuck on top of peach limbs; as giggly as she is gangly. To not love Annie would be a sin.

Eben notices the wooden bucket hanging in the back of the buggy that is used to fetch water for the horses. He unties it, turns it over to make a stool for Dicey. She then begins the struggle of moving into the seat. Her posture already stretches her scarred skin and now she is attempting to move vertically when horizontal movement looks excruciating. Eben realizes it will be easier to place his palms on her rump and lift her into the seat. The prospect of having his assistance construed improper, however, causes him consternation. He decides to assist her at her elbow. His exertion causes her to be levered sideways, with the elbow too relaxed and her shoulder being forced up. This is not the intended desire of his fulcrum, and worse yet, Dicey lets out a little "ooo," which makes him relax on the force resulting in a change in direction and Dicey falling back into him. It is going to be a long trip.

"Annie," Dicey begins, "you mind Miss Myrtle and make sure to help with sis and bubbers. OK?" Annie looks sadly at Dicey and runs up to the side of the wagon to hug her. Unable to reach that high, Eben walks over and lifts Annie up to Dicey. "I'll be back shoog," Dicey says, and Eben glows inside watching Dicey kiss her forehead.

Eben climbs into his side of the seat and exclaims loudly to the horses "Heeya," and soon the turning wheels lumber into their ruts. The trip up to Wilburton will take a day and half with the shade of the pine giving little relief from the humidity. Eben and Dicey talk an hour about a rabbit they saw and she lectures him about not eating rabbit in late summer because the fleas are bad and you can get the "fever." Dicey, who is normally shy, began her sentences with "Brother Eben." "Brother Eben, you know how poke salad is bad after it go to flower?" or "Brother Eben have you noticed that the persimmon harvest was bad because of the late frost?" Whatever she gathers to cook becomes a topic. Eben sits listening to his Choctaw Martha Stewart, mentally viewing her instructions in detail on how to kill, dress, and cook every animal from varmint to venison; conversations in Choctaw take twice as long.

After half a day Eben grows to respect Dicey so much that he will do anything for her but marry. He learns on this trip that so much of a person's worth is hidden by the pervasiveness of silence. Only a true Christian dares to challenge their own fears and move towards the perceived darkness of the unknown and listen to the unspoken depths of persons. People that are unfound friends because of the opaqueness created in fear. You can entertain angels.

Two hours on the other side of Yanush the two arrive at the home of Rhoda and Silas Anderson. Eben gives the standard greeting, reining in the horses simultaneously. After standing for nearly twenty minutes outside the fence, Silas smiles, nods, and waves for them to come in. Eben helps Dicey—who is already chattering with Rhoda about her pullets and the numerous bandy chickens running in the yard—down from the buggy. Eben fetches a bucket of water for the horse and then he loosens the armature from the harness. Halfway to their destination he is tired from being anxious.

The next morning, while they are departing, Silas waves, offering blessings for the journey. About mid-afternoon, after more conversation, they are wheeling into the bustling new commerce center of Wilburton. Eben is taken aback by the sheer number of attorneys that have moved into this rural city. In 1910, it seems with the coal mines came a flurry of conveyances and every new mineral asset had ten or more professionals to draw up abstracts. Each bank had at least one attorney for abstracts and they loaned them to the civic government to ensure every jot and tittle compliance of state law was afforded for Choctaws; compliance to ensure maximum fairness to all of Oklahoma's red children. Everything will eventually be stolen fairly. The state seal was adopted under the auspices of what it called a "peaceful conquest."

Eben scans the hanging signs, searching the painted calligraphy for "Smith." He arrives on the east side of town at the offices of Daniel Smith, Esq., built on Main Street with a rear access directly to the Latimer County Courthouse. The front of the office has a large picture glass that allows for an unobstructed view of the volumes of law books for the judiciary of Arkansas. Two oil paintings display locomotives traversing canyons, with white plumes trailing to disperse into billowing clouds that cushion the sunlit blue skies. The view from the street is to provide confidence in Smith's competence, as well as promote his American dream.

Eben unties the bucket, looking peripherally up the street at men congregated under awnings. He notices over a dozen eyes staring at him through windowfront reflections. Eben is aware that a full-blood carries as much social currency among whites as freedmen. He does not attempt to make eye contact with any of the standing men. He had considered going to the BIA with Annie's problem but they would send him to the appointed Choctaw Chief; stratification among the Choctaw reflects the American society around him in the new state. Eben knew the new chief would be none too sympathetic since the BIA like to appoint "their" kind of chief, a policy rubber stamp.

Internal prejudice within the tribe is rampant and he tells stories to friends about reading a letter from Chief Pitchlynn complaining to the government about education of the "Tubbies." Pithchlynn's elitism is towards Choctaws who carry traditional names that end in "Tabi," mispronounced "tubby," which means "to kill" or "killer." Tushkatabi would be translated "Warrior Killer." A Cherokee name like "Mankiller" would be "Hataktabi." Not that Choctaw society was ever egalitarian. A few hundred years earlier and Eben may have been from the Stinkard clan, a name that needs no explanation; missionary influence successfully suppressed tradition by replacing paradigms. Now there was no longer Greek or Jew, but pale and those cursed with the misery of melanin, where suffering was meted out based on degree of shade.

"Dicey when we get inside he may ask a question as to how I am related to Annie. You see, he may only speak to someone kin to Annie. When he speaks I will speak our tongue back to you to let you know what he's saying."

Eben holds her arm as they enter the door. The clerk inside insipidly glares at them for ringing the bell.

"May I help you?" The clerk's nasal voice leaks through his Ichabod Crane nose and gaunt face.

"We are here to see Mr. Smith regarding Annie Meshaya. This is her aunt Dicey Nuwa," Eben speaks, going over his English translation in his mind.

"Do you have an appointment? Mr. Smith is due in court and he is very busy." The normal routine is to delay by asking the party to have a seat; contamination of office property prevents the clerk from extending this courtesy to them. The reception wall is working when Mr. Smith steps into the foyer to investigate who is in his office.

Smith is five feet nine inches tall and in his early fifties. He is a handsome man by American standards, almost as handsome as Senator Owen. His vest is buttoned, with his tie pinned to his shirt by a Masons' triangle. He has a thin frame, with short brown hair crowning his shallow face. *He looks like a railroad lawyer* Eben thinks; of course among the Oklafalaya of this time period it is tough to tell white lawyers apart because they all look the same. You've seen one paddlefish, you've seen 'em all.

"So how is little Annie?" Smith remarks with concern, looking into Dicey's face.

"She's fine," Eben answers.

"I'm sorry, have we met?" Smith stares at Eben and they peer at each other through some invisible social caste.

"I'm an associate of Mrs. Nuwa here. She has asked me here to translate for her." With that Eben turns to Dicey and translates into Choctaw, "I told him who I am and that I am your tongue-speaker so that we can talk. He asked how Annie was and I told him she was fine. I think I will offer him *wak hakshun* (bull testicles) to eat." Dicey acknowledges this remark with an embarrassed grin and Eben turns back to Smith. He had translated directly to determine if Smith understood any of the Choctaw. Seeing no grimace he resumes his conversation. "Can we have a meeting with you regarding Annie? We've come nearly two days to speak to you."

Smith appears a little annoyed, or maybe that constipated look is just his resting appearance. At any rate, he turns to look at his clerk, who promptly hands him the calendar with court appearances, dockets, and trips to McAlester for the federal probate court.

"Hmmm," he says as he peruses the dates. "I'm afraid my clerk was correct in his information to you, I am in court later this afternoon, and in fact I should be heading that way soon. Maybe tomorrow morning, say before ten. Could we meet then?"

Smith appears to be accommodating, so Eben replies "Yes."

Eben casts a bemused glance at the clerk, who is adjusting the schedule on the calendar. Smith has already turned and walked back to his room during the rewriting. With nothing left to say, Eben and Dicey exit. Outside the wood-framed glass door Dicey asks questions, knowing it is safe to use Choctaw in the street.

"He seems to be a nice man?"

"Very busy," Eben smirks.

"He's got a lot of money doesn't he?" She makes a bowl with her hands.

"More than us," Eben helps Dicey into her seat.

"So you say," Dicey's response in Choctaw (Chikaiyo) is contextually a sarcastic remark like "No crap, or "Naw really?" Eben can't help but laugh.

"I bet he was gonna buy us dinner," Eben chortled. "Since we're about black, I bet he would have us clean the dishes when we were through."

Remarkably, Dicey grins at that comment and retrieves her toe sack from under her seat. She pulls out a cornhusk-rolled *banaha* (Choctaw Tamale) and fried salt pork, the Choctaw staples. She hands one to Eben, the whole time smiling as they begin backing away from the storefront, the horses ornery from the amount of work they have done the past two days. They wheel towards an Indian church outside of town, the direction of Red Oak.

CHAPTER 4

Prairie Oil and Gas is first mentioned in the 1904 report of the Indian Inspector for the Indian Territory. It seems the Cherokee Nation was not going to allow the laying of pipelines across citizens lands. As a result Prairie Oil managed to get Congress to approve the pipeline on March 11, 1904 (33 Stat., L., 65). The hubbub was caused because the inspector report of 1902 noted a large pool of oil being discovered at Red Fork in the Muscogee Nation. According to the inspector reports, in 1903, Cudahy Oil was working feverishly to tie down leases near Bartlesville. Cudahy Oil had been working with Cherokee Oil and Gas since 1897 and on the drilling of the Nellie Johnston well. The drilling company on the Nellie Johnstone well had attempted to drill at Red Fork and hit a dry well. It didn't matter the oil rush was on.

In the inspector report of 1902, Muscogee tribal citizens had issued 399 complaints of intruders on their allotments. Many of the intruders claimed they had legitimate leases with the Indians and would not leave. The federal government had to spend $15,000 to remove the intruders. It also had to pay for police to protect tribal members. Cushing is in Payne County. The Cushing Oil Field extended south into the Muscogee Nation, the tribal nation sits adjacent to Payne County. Payne County is named for the original intruder, David Payne. Payne had rode with Col. Custer in the Washita Massacre against the Cheyenne and Arapaho. Payne received money from railroads to pay for his Oklahoma Colony on Cherokee Land leading to the land run of 1889.

The Muscogee people say the word "Bear" as *No-coo-see* or *NaaKozee*, in the Muscogee tongue. It is a prominent name around Okmulgee, and is a significant clan as well. When the animals met in council in the time immemorial, it was the Bear that presided as the leader. It was there that the animal council voted for day and night to be equal like the rings on the tail of the Raccoon.

Katie Bear, called as a witness, being first duly sworn by L. W. Jones, Notary Public in and for Creek County, Oklahoma, testified as follows: Interpreted by Legus Brown.

EXAMINATION BY MR. MCGEE. (Hill Oil & Gas)

Q. What is your name? (Hill O&G $26,000,000 at stake)

A. Katie.

Q. You are also known as Katie Bear? (HOG$26MM)

A. I don't know. That is what they call me.

Q. Where do you live? (HOG$26MM)

A. Close to Deep Fork.

When the English made contact with the Muscogee Confederacy, they noted that their queendoms had stockades surrounding the community which sat on a river or a tributary. Thus the English called them "Creeks." Had the Muscogee built castles near moats, they could have become "Moats." The Muscogee say creek, *hut-chee.*

Q. How long have you lived there? (HOG$26MM)

A. Lived there a long time, ever since the war is over.

Q. That is down near Edna? (HOG$26MM)

A. Yes, sir, a little west, out that way.

Q. How old are you? (HOG$26MM)

A. I don't know just how old?

Q. Are you a citizen of the Creek Nation? (HOG$26MM)

A. Yes, sir.

Q. Did you know Ullie Eagle in her lifetime? (HOG$26MM)

A. Yes, sir.

Q. Do you know when she died? (HOG$26MM)

A. . . .

Ullie Eagle was an orphan when she received her allotment. The federal government was supposed to assign her a guardian for her estate. She is listed on Dawes census card 1357 with Sealie, age 90. Sealie's allotment suggest her roll number is 4337. Ullie is 4338. Sealie's allotment is located at Township 14 North Range 10 East in section 7. Katie Bear's roll number is 3983 and her allotment appears to be located at Township 14 North Range 10 East in section 29.

Q. Do you know Seelie or Ullie Eagle? (HOG$26MM)

A. I don't know what year she died?

Q. Was it in the spring or in the fall? (HOG$26MM)

A. Along about June?

Q. Who was she living with at the time she died? (HOG$26MM)

A. She was living with Seelie when she died.

Q. How far was that from where you live? (HOG$26MM)

A. Just close.

Q. How far, one-half mile? (HOG$26MM)

A. I don't know what a mile is; it was not very far from where I lived.

Q. What caused her death? (HOG$26MM)

A. There was two living together and they killed themselves. (HOG$26MM)s.

Q. Was anybody accused of the killing of Ullie Eagle?

A. No, there was just two there together.

Q. Were they both found dead? (HOG$26MM)

A. Yes, sir.

Q. Who was the other one beside Ullie? (HOG$26MM)

A. Hoktee.

In the Muscogee language you call girls *hokti*. Usually if it is a nickname there is an adjective that follows. *Hokti–lawnee* would be "Brown Girl." Katie would have known that since she requires a translator.

Q. Who was Ullie Eagle's mother? (HOG$26MM)

A. Toochie.

Q. Did you know Toochie? (HOG$26MM)

A. Yes, sir.

Q. Did she live with you? (HOG$26MM)

A. Yes, sir.

Q. When did she die? (HOG$26MM)

A. Either eight or nine.

Q. (TO INTERPRETER) Ask her if she means 1898 or 1899. (HOG$26MM)

A. Don't know.

Q. Did she die before Ullie? (HOG$26MM)

A. Toochie died before Ullie.

Q. Who was Ullie's father? (HOG$26MM)

A. David.

Q. David Eagle? (HOG$26MM)

A. Fellow by the name of David, and father of this child.

Q. Do you know whether Ullie Eagle had any brothers or sisters? (HOG$26MM)

A. No, sir, not any.

Q. Did Toochie have any children except Ullie? (HOG$26MM)

A. Yes, there was some but they died.

Q. How many? (HOG$26MM)

A. Just two.

Q. Did they die before Ullie died? (HOG$26MM)

A. Toochie died when this child was little baby. She kept it and raised it, and then went and married again.

Q. Did these two children that Toochie had die before or after Ullie died? (HOG$26MM)

A. They died before Ullie.

Q. Did Dave Eagle have one other child? (HOG$26MM)

A. No, sir, not any.

Q. Do you know when David Eagle died? (HOG$26MM)

A. No, sir, I don't know.

Q. Do you know whether he died before or after Toochie died? (HOG$26MM)

A. Dave died before Toochie did.

Q. Do you know how long before? (HOG$26MM)

A. About two years.

Q. Did Ullie Eagle ever have any children? (HOG$26MM)

A. No, sir.

Q. How old was Ullie Eagle when she died? (HOG$26MM)

A. About eight.

Q. Did you know when Ullie was born? (HOG$26MM)

A. I don't know, never kept any record.

Q. Do you know who Toochie's mother was? (HOG$26MM)

A. My sister.

Q. What was her name? (HOG$26MM)

A. Secehuy.

Q. Who was Toochie's father? (HOG$26MM)

A. Hotulke Fixico.

Hotulke is a derivative word *ho-dull-ee,* which means "wind." The Wind Clan among the Muscogee is among the most prominent. One Muscogee word for the creator is *Hesaketvmase* which means "giver of breath." When the creator formed the first humans on the mound, the creator blew into the nostrils of the humans, giving them life. The wind came from the east to fill the first breath. Thus the sacred direction of the morning sun and why the entrance to Muscogee churches face east.

Q. Did Toochie have any brothers or sisters? (HOG$26MM)

A. No, sir.

Q. When did Secehuy die? (HOG$26MM)

A. I don't know.

Q. Did she die before or after Toochie died? (HOG$26MM)

A. Mother died before Toochie; she was a little baby and she raised it.

Q. Do you mean Toochie was a little baby? (HOG$26MM)

A. Toochie died then she took the little baby and raised it.

Q. Did Secehuy have any children? (HOG$26MM)

A. Yes, sir, has three, but other two died and Toochie died away afterwards; after she got to be a woman.

Q. The other two died before Toochie? (HOG$26MM)

A. Yes, sir.

Q. Were Santale Fixico and Secehuy ever married? (HOG$26MM)

A. Yes, sir.

Q. How long did they live together? (HOG$26MM)

A. Lived together a long time.

Q. About how long? (HOG$26MM)

A. Lived together a long time, don't know how many years.

Q. Which one of them died first? (HOG$26MM)

A. Secehuy died first.

Q. How long after that did Santale Fixico die? (HOG$26MM)

A. I don't know just how long afterwards.

Q. Who was Secehuy's mother? (HOG$26MM)

A. Ficonne.

Q. Who was Secehuy's father? (HOG$26MM)

A. Miccapeka.

Q. Did they both die before Secehuy died? (HOG$26MM)

A. Secehuy died before the father did. The mother died first, Secehuy died and the father afterwards.

Q. When did the father die? (HOG$26MM)

A. Died shortly after the Civil War was over.

Q. These two were you father and mother? (HOG$26MM)

A. Yes, sir, that was my father and mother.

Q. Did you have any other brothers and sisters, except Secehuy? (HOG$26MM)

A. No, sir, there was no others. Just us two.

Q. Did the father have any other children except Katie and Secehuy? (HOG$26MM)

A. No, sir, not any.

Q. Did you know who David Eagle's mother was? (HOG$26MM)

A. Leshka.

Q. Do you know who David Eagle's father was? (HOG$26MM)

A. Hathan Harjo.

Q. Did David Eagle have any brothers or sisters? (HOG$26MM)

A. Yes, he had some but don't know the names.

Q. How many? (HOG$26MM)

A. Don't know how many, just one brother by the name of Kasac . . .only one she remembers.

Q. Is he dead or alive? (HOG$26MM)

A. Yes, sir.

Q. When did he die? (HOG$26MM)

A. I don't know.

Q. Was he married when he died? (HOG$26MM)

A. Yes had a wife, but she died and I don't know when it was.

Q. Did she die before or after he did? (HOG$26MM)

A. The man died first and the women died afterwards.

Q. Did they have any children? (HOG$26MM)

A. Yes, sir, they had some children but don't know what became of them.

Q. Do you know the names? (HOG$26MM)

A. I don't know.

Q. Do you know whether they are still alive? (HOG$26MM)

A. No, sir.

Q. Do you know the names? (HOG$26MM)

A. I don't know.

Q. You know whether they are still alive? (HOG$26MM)

A. No, sir.

Somewhere in this transcript the interview changed. It is difficult to go back and examine who was conducting cross-examination.

Q. Are you sure it wasn't June that Ullie died? (McMahan O&G $26,000,000 at stake)

A. I'm not sure it was that month but it was about that.

Q. Was it in the early summer or late in the summer? (MOG$26MM)

A. About the middle of summer I guess.

Q. Katie, did you ever know one by the name of Winney Tiger? (MOG$26MM)

A. Yes, sir.

Q. Is she a sister of David Eagle? (MOG$26MM)

A. Yes, sir.

Q. Did you ever know an Indian by the name of Timmie Jessie? (MOG$26MM)

A. Yes, sir, moved away afterwards and heard he died.

Q. Was Timmie Jessie brother of Toochie? (MOG$26MM)

A. Timmie Jessie died.

Q. Is Timmie Jessie brother of Toochie? (MOG$26MM)

A. Yes, Toochie was his sister. Timmie Jessie died.

Q. Which died first: Toochie or Timmie Jessie? (MOG$26MM)

A. Don't remember which died first.

Q. Toochie died before the girl? (MOG$26MM)

A. Yes, Toochie.

Q. Timmie died after girl, didn't he? (MOG$26MM)

A. Timmie died before Ullie.

Q. Does she know when Timmie died or where? (MOG$26MM)

A. No, sir.

Q. You know an Indian woman by the name of Nellie Fish? (MOG$26MM)

A. No, sir.

Q. You know women by the name of Nellie down by Wetumka? (MOG$26MM)

In Muscogee "water" is said *Owa,* and thus town names like Wetumka actually would be said *Owatumka* or "thundering water" for a waterfall. *Owaleetka* would be "running water." During the Muscogee Confederacy the town of Wetumka was in the Wewoka district. Wewoka is *Owawoka* or "barking water." The tribal town, queendom, Thlopthlocco bears its name for the sound that lily pads make on water when gentle winds cause them to dance—thlop, thlop, thlop. The queendom Fish Pond is named for the pond that results from the earth being dug to build the large ceremonial mounds in the old lands. On the top of those mounds stood the house for the Micco Leader. On smaller mounds stood a house to hold the bones of the ancestors. Earth to Sky, Water to Wind.

A. No, sir, I do not.

Q. Did Timmie Jessie have a sister? (MOG$26MM)

A. I don't know.

Q. I will ask you another question: Didn't Toochie have another sister by the name of Nellie Fish? (MOG$26MM)

A. No, sir.

Q. If you have a sister? What was her sister's name? (MOG$26MM)

A. She had one by the name of Jar Fisher.

Q. The Toochie have a sister by the name of Nellie, just Nellie? (MOG$26MM)

A. No, sir.

Q. Did you ever hear of this woman Nellie Fish down about Wetumka or Weleetka? (MOG$26MM)

A. No, sir.

Q. Did you ever hear of this woman, Nellie, claiming to be the sister of Toochie? (MOG$26MM)

A. No, sir, I do not.

Q. What is your son's name? Marchie? (MOG$26MM)

A. Yes, sir.

Q. Does he live with you? (MOG$26MM)

A. Yes, sir.

Q. You remember along last spring winter of talking to me about this matter, this man here was interpreter, (indicating Roy E. Scales) at your house? (MOG$26MM)

A. No, sir, I don't remember.

Q. Of talking about Nellie Fish, Timmie, Jessie, and Ullie? (MOG$26MM)

A. I forgot.

Q. So remember we actually talk about this matter when we came over to the store where there was a notary public, over at Edna? (MOG$26MM)

A. Yes . . . she remembers now.

Q. Ask her if I didn't ask her a question then about Nellie Fish. (MOG$26MM)

A. I don't remember now.

Q. Marchie was there at the same time? (MOG$26MM)

A. Yes, sir.

Q. Did you state there that Toochie had one brother, Timmie Jessie? (MOG$26MM)

A. Yes, that was the brother, son of Katcoce, she heard it was.

Q. Didn't you tell us at the same time that Nellie Fish was a sister of Timmie Jessie, brother of Toochie? (MOG$26MM)

A. She don't know for sure herself. She heard there was a sister by that name. She never saw the party.

Q. She heard there was a sister by that name? (MOG$26MM)

A. Yes, sir.

Q. Did you ever see Katcoce? (MOG$26MM)

A. No, sir.

Q. Wasn't that the general understanding or talk among the Indians and the general reputation that Nellie Fish was a sister of Toochie?

A. No, sir, don't remember.

Q. You had heard and understood that Nellie Fish was a sister of Toochie yourself? (MOG$26MM)

A. No, sir.

Q. Ask her if it is not a fact that Nellie Fish was a sister of Toochie. (MOG$26MM)

Mr. McGee. We wish to object to that unless it was shown by the general reputation in the community.

Mr. Walker. Note your objection.

A. I don't remember.

Q. There may be some children by Timmie Jessie? (MOG$26MM)

A. I don't know.

Q. What I'm asking you about is Nellie. (MOG$26MM)

A. No, sir, I don't know about that.

Q. Did you tell me through Roy Scales here as interpreter, when you and Marchie were together talking about this matter, tell me Nellie was a sister to Toochie? (MOG$26MM)

A. No, sir, I don't remember telling you that because I don't really know whether or not she had any by that name or not. She heard that but don't know for sure herself; of course there was some land deal, I guess you was trying to buy, and it was about the land sale you were questioning her of relatives of this party, if she don't know for sure; she don't know much about it anyway.

Q. Did she tell the people in this land sale that Nellie Fish claimed to be a sister? (MOG$26MM)

A. No, she don't really know the relatives of that party at all.

Q. She does know that Timmie Jessie was a brother? (MOG$26MM)

A. Yes, sir.

Q. Do you know David Eagle? (MOG$26MM)

A. Yes, sir.

Q. The David Eagle have a sister by the name of Winney Tiger? (MOG$26MM)

A. Yes, sir.

Q. Is she living or dead? (MOG$26MM)

A. There was one by that name but she died. (MOG$26MM)

Q. Did she have any children? (MOG$26MM)

A. She left some children, don't know whether they are better not.

Q. Do you know any of their names? (MOG$26MM)

A. No, sir.

Q. Is Suzy Tiger one of them, or do you know? (MOG$26MM)

A. She may be one of them but I don't know.

RE-EXAMINATION BY MR. MCGEE

Q. Who was Timmie Jessie's mother? (HOG$26MM)

A. I don't know.

Q. Do you know who the father was? (HOG$26MM)

A. Santale Fixico.

Q. Do you know when Timmie Jessie died? (HOG$26MM)

A. I don't know.

Q. What did Scales say to you at the time of the conversation they were asking you about? (HOG$26MM)

A. I don't remember. I have forgotten. March may know, but he is not here. I don't know anything about it. I have forgotten.

Q. Did you ever hear anything about Nellie Fish being a brother of Toochie before you had that conversation with Scales? (HOG$26MM)

A. No, sir, I did not.

Q. Did you ever hear anything about Timmie Jessie being a brother of Toochie before you had that conversation with Scales? (HOG$26MM)

A. Yes, sir.

Q. You don't know whether Timmie Jessie died before or after Ullie died, do you? (HOG$26MM)

A. Timmie Jessie may have died first, but don't know the exact date.

Q. Were you present at the burial of Toochie? (HOG$26MM)

A. Yes, sir, I was present. She died at my house.

Q. Were you present at the burial of Secehuy? (HOG$26MM)

A. Yes, sir, I was home.

Q. Was Santale Fixico present at the burial of Secehuy? (HOG$26MM)

A. I was present when he died.

Q. Did you stay around there after her death? (HOG$26MM)

A. Yes, he was there a while, he went away, and heard he died, but I don't know just where he died.

Q. Did you ever see him again after he went away that time? (HOG$26MM)

A. No, sir, never saw him since.

Q. Did you ever hear from him? (HOG$26MM)

A. Yes, hear he was up to Raprako (Thlopthlocco).

Thlopthlocco Queendom during the Muscogee Confederacy was located in the Deep Fork District named for the river and the boundaries. Had the state of Sequoyah passed it would probably be located in Arbeka County. Instead it became Okfuskee County. Thlophlocco in the 1930s had the privilege of having a Mekko (Leader) named Roley Canard appointed as the Mekko of the Muscogee Nation. He attempted to reorganize 32 Tribal Towns back into the Muscogee Confederacy based on their Constitution. He met opposition because the BIA would not allow for the Muscogee to exclude the freedman. Solicitors' opinions asserted that the House of Kings and House of Warriors had signed the 1866 Treaty, wherein the Muscogee Nation adopted the Freedmen. As a result, Roley had Dr. Morris Opler conduct an analysis of the confederacy. Opler concluded that the Tribal Towns as the original form of Muscogee Government could form their own distinct governments as "Bands" under the Oklahoma Indian Welfare Act. Thlophtlocco would become the first Tribal Town with federal recognition. Alabama-Quassarte and Kialegee would follow suit. Nellie Fish the aunt of Ullie Eagle, was matrilineal Kialegee.

Q. Where is that place? (HOG$26MM)

A. Out that way.

Q. How long after he left there before you heard he was dead? (HOG$26MM)

A. I don't remember. Never thought about such things being brought up back to my mind. Never kept a record of it.

RE-CROSS EXAMINATION BY MR. ROGERS (McMan Oil & Gas, i.e., Chapman-McFarlin)

Q. Is that place she spoke about (Thlopthlocco), Raprako (Indian Town), that is where Timmie Jessie was? (MOG$26MM)

A. I don't know. Timmie Jessie lived there.

Q. Is that where Timmie Jessie lived? (MOG$26MM)

A. Yes, sir.

Q. You say you never heard of Nellie Fish until Scales was out there talking about it? (MOG$26MM)

A. No, sir. Don't know that party, and don't know yet.

Q. You know Mr. Thrift, a lawyer that used to live here in Sapulpa, now lives in Bristow? (MOG$26MM)

A. No, sir.

Q. Do you know L. B. Jackson, a lawyer that used to be Thrift's partner? (MOG$26MM)

L. B. Jackson, in the December 1916 *Oil Trade Journal*, is listed as an Oil Producer and one of the Vice-Presidents of Union National Bank of Tulsa, Oklahoma. His law office was in Sapulpa. He and H. H. Rogers were listed as V. P. of the Bank.

A. No, sir.

Q. Didn't you go to their office here in Sapulpa in this building and ask them to bring a suit against Purdy to cancel a deed made to Purdy, about a year ago? (MOG$26MM)

A. No, sir.

Q. And you didn't give them a statement of facts about these heirs? (MOG$26MM)

A. I don't remember.

Q. Didn't you give Thrift a statement about who was the heirs and told him all about Ullie matter? (MOG$26MM)

A. I don't know who you are talking about.

Q. I am talking about a lawyer here in Sapulpa. (MOG$26MM)

Sapulpa is named for a former Speaker from the House of Warriors. He had served in the Confederacy and was a man of significant means. Sapulpa was in the Okmulgee District of the Muscogee Confederacy and had Sequoyah become a state his town would be in Euchee (Yuchi) County. The Euchee do not speak Muscogee, they speak Euchee, which is not Muscogean. They joined the confederacy after the Creek and Cherokee wars. This is not unique. Tucabatchee is a mother town. Tucabatchee has a unique relation with the Shawnee who are Algonquian, yet the Tucabatchee speak Muscogean. The Euchee language is an unique and unlike any other tribal language group. The Euchee speak of themselves as "children of the Sun."

A. No, sir.

Q. Did you ever hire a lawyer to look after the Ullie matter for you? (MOG$26MM)

A. No, sir.

Q. Did you ever talk to any lawyers here about hiring them? (MOG$26MM)

A. No, sir.

Q. You know who the wife of Timmie Jessie was? (MOG$26MM)

A. I know her, but don't know the name.

Q. Was it Elizabeth? (MOG$26MM)

A. Yes, sir.

Q. Elizabeth Spaniard? (MOG$26MM)

A. Yes, that is the name.

CHAPTER 5

In 1907, the state of Oklahoma was founded by the combination of Indian Territory with Oklahoma Territory. A mock wedding was conducted in Guthrie where a Cowboy married a lady representing an Indian Princess. Had she been named Pocahontas then the Cowboy would have no doubt been named John Smith. The nuptials were practically a shotgun wedding. Here is hegemony in its full bloom. The immigrant culture was always seeking to legitimize the taking of tribal land. By making Pocahontas a princess and marrying her, a landed gentry, in effect, automatically made her property his property. Virginia soil as a duty of bride price. The Okies were recreating the same imagery. Now the Cherokee woman became property of the Cowboy. So all of her little red children were now under his authority. To say that the Cowboy was an abusive sack of crap is beyond the point. Her body was his property and if he felt like beating her for being obstinate, he could. If he felt like raping her, he could. Women did not get half in a divorce in 1907; they could leave the marriage, just without taking any of their property and most likely their children.

Adair County would have originally been under the protection of the Cherokee Nation's Going Snake District. It would have become Flint County in the Indian state of Sequoyah.

Josephine Perry was probably an Osage or Ponca girl, and after her death was owed $4,227.52. A house that cost $3,200 in 1915 would in 2015 cost $177,600. In fact, housing cost for any orphan in 1910 with a dollar would be worth $89.68 in 2021.

Atoka County would have originally been under the protection of the Choctaw Nation's Pushmataha District of Jacks Fork County and Atoka County. It would have become Bixby County in the Indian state of Sequoyah.

In 1907, Kate Barnard (Catholic) was elected the Commissioner of Charities and Corrections. She became the first woman elected to a major office in any state in the nation. She was elected and could not even vote. Within three years of statehood she began uncovering the names of many orphans like Ullie; Kate catalogued them by county and how much they were owed from their royalties with the dollar amounts in her reports. There were too many orphans for one woman to calculate. In her fourth annual report for the period of October 1, 1911 to October 1, 1912 she began her exhaustive lists:

ADAIR COUNTY

Jessi Fixin

Susie Blackbird

George Blackbird

ALFALFA COUNTY

Josephine Perry, $4,227.52. ($379,123.99)

Marie Orin Thompson $2,200.00 ($197,296)

ATOKA COUNTY

Alfred Wilkin

Henry Wilkin

John Wilkin

Ramond Wilkin

CHAPTER 6

The camphouses provided to Eben and Dicey are more than accommodating. Many camphouses are simple ten-by-ten sheds, with a large porch and galvanized roof sheeting. The houses are roughed in, which means you can see the frame inside the shell. They are better than a tent, not much more opulent than a henhouse. Pastor Meshaya doesn't refrain from teasing Eben that he might get the Holy Spirit staying at a Baptist church. Eben is quick to respond that the pastor should be thankful that the spirit has finally come to his church, since Baptists seem confused about true grace. Denominational jabs done with love lead the men to spend the evening swapping stories and laughing with intensity. The grown men's bellies dance like jelly during their laughter. Mrs. Meshaya makes some nuanced derogatory jokes about males that make Dicey smile. The laughter mkaes the night pass too quickly.

Eben is up at first light and already the day is proving to be difficult; the horse will not open his mouth to take the bit. "Now look here, we have an important meeting and I don't have the patience to argue with you all morning. Stop swaying your head." Again the horse is nonresponsive, like Balaam's donkey. "Father God, please make this horse open its mouth," Eben breathes in exasperation, trying to keep his aspiration from framing cuss words at church. The horse's head goes straight down to avoid the bit again and Eben puts it at the mouth and yanks up hard. The horse, now with bit in, gnaws at the metal in defiance, swishing tail displaying his grumpiness. Eben, in hindsight, will become aware that things are always more difficult on important days, especially when a horse has never been past twenty miles.

Eben secures the tug on the buggy and Dicey unexpectedly helps cinch the harness. "This old horse fussy this morning?" Dicey says as she shadows her smile.

"I think it's used to traveling a few days a week, and then having time off for three," Eben replies. After getting the harness secure he begins the routine of loading to ride; bucket, Dicey, bucket, untie reins, and then hop in seat. Upon arrival, step from seat, tie reins, bucket, Dicey, bucket.

Coming into Wilburton from the east and the morning sun is bright on the side of the buildings, causing a brick glare. Shadows from the horse and buggy push forward like a compass arrow, pointing true west. "Go west and find your dreams young man" were the appellations of the generation; unless you are already part of the west, then it's "move your ass, Indian." No red devils in the Manifest Destiny painting unless they are fleeing the great white light.

As they pull in front of the office, Eben completes the arrival routine. He limps to Dicey's side, stepping hard to get blood flowing to slumbered toes lacking blood from the buggy seat. "Dicey, if I fall just don't let the horse step on me. I don't think a doctor will see me here in this town."

"Maybe to castrate you," she says, covering her smile with her hand and laughing. Eben looks up and shakes his head, laughing.

"Well, please don't call for one in that case," he says as he secures Dicey's arm.

They step up to the door of the office and sit on the bench in front. Within thirty minutes the "hospitable" clerk arrives on foot with a disgruntled look on his face. Pointedly he jabs, "Your appointment with Mr. Smith is not until later this morning is it?"

Feigning politeness, Eben counters, "The roosters were up and so we thought we better be here. Too many things can happen in a morning that could make us late."

"Well, you'll just have to wait." The clerk turns the key and enters the office, then pushes the door shut, making the glass rattle a little.

"I guess we aren't going to get coffee out of him," Eben smirks.

Eben and Dicey talk in Choctaw, describing the clerk's gaunt appearance. They discuss his possible origins in Kansas or somewhere that hates Indians. They discuss why white people hate Choctaw, why the God of love tolerates human hatred. They then liken animal personalities to some people, and even discuss the town store fronts—anything to occupy the time. At one point Dicey calls the clerk Sheki, which means "buzzard"; she calls him that probably because of his thin bowed neck, or maybe it is his nose. You can hook his legs to a horse, stand on his head, and plow with his sharp German nose.

Buzzard peeps his head out. "Mr. Smith will see you now."

Eben helps Dicey up and then holds the door while she enters. As they walk one of the new floorboards squeaks and Dicey remarks "*Hoonkso shoowa*," which means "stinky fart." Eben grinns as he follows her around the corner to Smith's office. As they enter, Smith is sitting reviewing a brief and does not look up. His office is frosted-glass encased. Casings at the top open to allow air flow from the front office through to the back.

Smith peers up from his papers and says, "Now, what was so important that you had to see me?"

Eben reads faces well and senses that this is not going to be a meeting with quid pro quo. "Ms. Nuwa received this letter from your office and was curious about Annie's royalties, where they are from and things of that nature."

"Hasn't the Bureau of Indian Affairs been in contact with you regarding this?" Smith quizzes.

Eben shakes his head and then startles himself when he says, "*Kiyo*, I mean no."

"Well this issue has already been through a hearing before Judge Skinner and his court appointed my office to handle the specifics. I have transmitted the notice to the Agency Superintendent down in Talihina. I'm sure he has filed the information with the Muskogee Office by now. If you haven't received notice it's probably just a matter of time." Smith finishes speaking and his mouth is pinched slightly, ready for volley two.

Eben turns to Dicey and repeats the information in Choctaw. Dicey listens intently and asks in their language, "Is the money from her dad's land?"

"Dicey wants to know if the money is from Annie's dad's land."

"The Probate on that is being completed now and I know that Annie is the sole heir. Her dad's land is the source of the income, yes."

Eben looked at Dicey and nods. Dicey then asks "Did her daddy have coal on his land?"

"Dicey wants to know if there is coal on the land."

"I believe so."

Eben indicates yes again. "Can some of it be used for her, to help buy her some shoes?" Eben turns and relays the statement back to Smith.

"I'm sure we can make some of it available for that kind of stuff, but you have to understand that the revenue from the land is put in a bank account for her to have when she turns eighteen. Of course the funds provide for other services to take care of her until that time. We can't just let anyone come in here and spend her money." Smith leans back as though having pronounced judgment.

Eben looks at Smith's face and feels an indignant wind rolling in his lungs. His mind rushes and he looks down at the floor to change the visual information, trying to refocus and not erupt. "If the money is Annie's why doesn't her aunt get to decide what is best for her?"

"Excuse me?" Smith is startled that anyone would question him, especially a dark-skinned Indian.

"Why can't Dicey have enough to provide for Annie, say on a monthly schedule so that she can have nice clothes, some shoes, and other necessities?"

"What's in it for you, boy? You takin' care of the aunt to get a hold of the money?"

"I'm here to help Dicey understand," Eben fights hard to contain his man.

"Looks funny. All of a sudden she shows up with a man I ain't ever seen, all worried about money that's taken care of. You need to buy some of that Choc Beer?"

Eben sits back, realizing that he is being baited. Why? He sits back, returning a pinched smile to Smith. Turning to Dicey, and without speaking, he stands and she joins him, perplexed.

Smith, obviously relishing the sanctimonious torment, adds, "I'm gonna talk to Judge Skinner about Annie needing to go to Wheelock. I think boarding school will better serve her interest."

Dicey stares directly at Eben's face, trying to ask with her eyes what is going on. Eben walks them outside and loads Dicey into the buggy. After untying from the hitch he boards his side, "Dicey it looks like the white man is hiding something and he may try to move Annie away to Wheelock."

"*Kiyo*! NO! NO!" She moans.

"I know, I'm so sorry. But I bet he gets some kind of order from the court that will allow him to do that." Eben tries to clarify the full conversation in the office. Dicey looks dazed, staring at the store windows as they start away to return home.

"That man doesn't want Annie to be taken care of, does him? He just wants her money. Do you think he would just keep her money and let her stay with me with no change, kind of like we didn't even come here?" She searches for hope in his face.

"While you went off to sleep last night, Pastor Meshaya came and told me something that worried me. He said his little brother, Fawni, had gotten picked up a few months back for public drunkenness, and when he was laying on his pallet the next morning he could see Smith and Judge Skinner having a conversation with the sheriff outside the jail. He knew who Judge Skinner was because he appeared before him later that day. He said Smith was sitting behind a table reading law books when the Judge called his name on another case. He was sitting in the back row with two other fellas waiting for the fourth guy to have his turn at the bench. One of those men called Smith Cotton Mouth, and Fawni asked why he called him that and the other prisoner said cause you don't get a warning like you do from a rattle snake is what he meant, but you get bit the same, don't you?"

CHAPTER 7

Okmulgee is the historic capitol of the Muscogee people in Oklahoma. "Boiling water" is the translation of the capitol name, indicating food preparation. During the ceremonial feasts hominy is boiled with pork to make a popular dish. Ocmulgee was a Queendom in Georgia where a beautiful mound stands for Macon tourists to see. It was suggested by antiquarians that it was not built by the Muscogee. Mound-builders were thought to be everyone from the Welsh to the Vikings. Andrew Jackson favored attributing the great mound-building cultures to someone other than the primitive tribes of the southeast. Making the tribes guilty of dispossession of a greater culture played in the narrative for the new nation to provide a rationale for removal.

Okmulgee in Oklahoma would become the site of one of the first functioning oil refineries in Oklahoma. The wealth in this community was so opulent that the Muscogee people were forced to sell their historic downtown sandstone capitol building to the state. Ironically, that capitol building would have to be bought back by them a century later with a price tag of millions, whereas the Federal Government forced them to liquidate it to the city for pennies on the dollar.

In 1895, Congress allowed for the survey of all tribal properties for allotment. The surveyors also noted minerals. Indian interpreters could get one dollar for every lease signature and up to two dollars and fifty cents for contracts for those minerals. Tams Bixby, the chairman of the allotment act, was busy securing leases for himself after allotting land, because he and the surveyor, after all, knew where a lot of the oil lay. Robert Owens had been the Indian Agent for the Cherokee, Muscogee, Choctaw, Chickasaw, and Seminole nations. He soon became the first senator from Oklahoma. He had been busy since 1902 having himself appointed guardian for Indian orphans and collecting fees in the form of land. It was as Senator that he ensured the protection of allotments, and thus protection from theft was lifted. Okmulgee was a boomtown then. Motey Tiger, a chief of the Muscogee, called Owens a snake in a public speech. Lawyers in the formative years of the state made millions off of oil and land. The actions of those lawyers was much like that of mercenaries. In feudal terms, they were Knights of the Judiciary.

P. E. McGee was just another judicial knight for Hill Oil & Gas. Hill Oil was owned by an Ohioan named William Carnill. McGee was the Vice President of the company. The oil company was like many smaller independents, clawing and hustling for Indian oil leases.

Marsie Harry, called as a witness, being first duly sworn by L.W. Jones, Notary Public, in and for Creek County, Oklahoma, testified as follows: Legus Brown sworn as interpreter.

EXAMINATION BY MR. MCGEE.

Q. State your name. (HOG$26MM)

A. Marsie Harry.

Q. Where do you live? (HOG$26MM)

A. West of Beggs. Twelve miles.

Q. How long have you lived there? (HOG$26MM)

A. About forty years, a long time.

Q. How old are you? (HOG$26MM)

A. About fifty or sixty years.

Q. Are you any relation to David Harry who testified a while ago? (HOG$26MM)

A. No, sir.

Q. Did you know Ullie Eagle in her lifetime? (HOG$26MM)

A. Yes, sir.

Witness testified from this point without an interpreter.

Q. Where did Ullie Eagle live? (HOG$26MM)

A. Quarter of a mile from my place.

Q. When did Ullie Eagle die? (HOG$26MM)

A. I don't know.

Q. Were you there at the time she died? (HOG$26MM)

A. Yes, sir.

Q. What time of the year was it? (HOG$26MM)

A. I don't know

Q. Was it about peach time? (HOG$26MM)

A. No, sir.

Q. You don't remember whether it was in the summer, fall, or spring? (HOG$26MM)

A. It was in the summer.

Q. Was it in the early summer or late summer? (HOG$26MM)

A. Late, I think.

Q. You don't know what month it was? (HOG$26MM)

A. No, sir.

Q. You know where she is buried? (HOG$26MM)

A. Yes, sir.

Q. Where?

A. Half-mile from my home.

Q. Do you know whether or not there's any kind of a tombstone there? (HOG$26MM)

A. No, sir.

Mr. Walker. Do you mean there is a tombstone at her grave?

A. No, sir.

Mr. McGee. Is there a tombstone at Ullie Eagle's grave? (HOG$26MM)

A. No, sir.

Q. Do you know who Ullie Eagle's mother was? (HOG$26MM)

A. Yes, sir.

Q. Who was it? (HOG$26MM)

A. Toochie.

Q. Do you know the father? (HOG$26MM)

A. Who?

Q. David Eagle? (HOG$26MM)

A. Yes.

Q. Did Toochie die before or after Ullie Eagle? (HOG$26MM)

A. Toochie died first and then the mammy.

Q. to David Eagle die first or after Toochie died? (HOG$26MM)

A. He died first, I think.

Q. Do you know who Toochie's mother was? (HOG$26MM)

A. I never seen them. I heard it.

Q. Who was it? (HOG$26MM)

A. Chehoche. I heard the name; never saw her.

Q. Do you know who Toochie's father was? (HOG$26MM)

A. No, sir.

Q. Do you know when Secehuy died? (HOG$26MM)

A. No, sir.

Q. Did Ullie Eagle have any brothers or sisters? (HOG$26MM)

A. Yes, sir.

Q. How many? (HOG$26MM)

A. Two of them, I think, died long ago; Winney Tiger is a sister.

Q. Do you mean Winney Tiger is a sister of Ullie Eagle? (HOG$26MM)

A. Yes, sir. David Eagle's sister is Winney Tiger.

Q. Did Ullie Eagle have any brothers or sisters? (HOG$26MM)

A. Yes, sir.

Q. Were they living at the time Ullie Eagle died? (HOG$26MM)

A. . . .

Q. Were these brothers and sisters of Ullie Eagle living at the time Ullie died? (HOG$26MM)

A. Ullie Eagle?

Q. Did Ullie Eagle have any brothers or sisters living when she died? (HOG$26MM)

A. No, sir.

Q. Did any of her brothers or sisters have any children? (HOG$26MM)

A. No, sir.

Q. Did they all die when small? (HOG$26MM)

A. Yes, sir.

Q. Did Ullie Eagle have any children? (HOG$26MM)

A. No, sir.

Q. How old was Ullie Eagle when she died? (HOG$26MM)

A. About so high (witness indicating) pretty near ten years old.

Q. You don't know when Ullie Eagle was born? (HOG$26MM)

A. Yes, sir.

Q. How long ago? (HOG$26MM)

A. I don't know, about ten years now. I don't know exactly.

Q. Did Toochie have any brothers or sisters? (HOG$26MM)

A. Yes, two small, both died long time ago.

Q. What were her sisters' names? (HOG$26MM)

A. I don't know.

Q. Did the others die before Toochie died? (HOG$26MM)

A. Toochie died first.

Q. You say Toochie had some brothers or sisters? (HOG$26MM)

A. I don't know.

Q. Did Secehuy have any brothers or sisters? (HOG$26MM)

A. I don't know.

Q. Who was Ullie Eagle living with at the time she died? (HOG$26MM)

A. A grandma, and when grandma died the uncle took her; this old lady her son took her?

Q. What lady do you mean? (HOG$26MM)

A. Katie.

Q. This a lady that is here? (HOG$26MM)

A. Yes, sir.

Q. Did you say David Eagle had some brothers or sisters? (HOG$26MM)

A. Yes, sir.

Q. How many? (HOG$26MM)

A. Two sisters and one brother.

Q. What were their names? (HOG$26MM)

A. One sister Polly, one Tiger Eagle.

Q. What was the other one? (HOG$26MM)

A. That is all.

Q. Are they both dead? (HOG$26MM)

A. Yes, sir.

Q. Die before or after David died? (HOG$26MM)

A. The sister died first, David right behind.

Q. Did the other brother die before David? (HOG$26MM)

A. Yes, sir.

Q. You say whether or not Toochie had any brothers or sisters? (HOG$26MM)

A. No, sir.

Q. You don't know? (HOG$26MM)

A. No.

Cross-examination by Mr. Rogers (McMan Oil & Gas, i.e., Chapman-McFarlin)

Henry Rogers was a knight for McMan Oil Company. As mentioned, he first hung his shingle in the city of Wewoka, Barking Waters, which is the capitol of the Seminole Nation. Rogers then joined McMan Oil down the road in Holdenville, which is the southernmost city of the Muscogee Nation. In fact Rogers had been the land man for McMan in Hughes and Seminole counties. Holdenville is nine miles from Wewoka and nineteen from Wetumka. In 1897, the oil boom in Wewoka district of the Muscogee and Seminole nations turned lawless and ruthless. It got so bad that two Seminole boys who were accused of raping and killing a white woman named Laird were captured and killed. It wasn't a normal lynching though—three hundred residents of Maud cheered while the boys were chained to a tree and burned alive. The federal government was forced to investigate. Up the road from Wewoka in Cromwell the boomtown became so lawless that a former Federal Marshal named Bill Tilghman was sent in to rein in the prostitution and illicit liquor trade in 1924. Bill successfully extorted enough money from the whorehouses that he had a run-in with another Federal officer sent in to shut down the bootleggers and in the exchange the famous Tilghman caught a bullet.

Q. David Eagle have a sister by the name of Winney Tiger? (MOG$26MM)

A. Yes, sir.

Q. Living or dead? (MOG$26MM)

A. Dead.

Q. Did she have any children? (MOG$26MM)

A. Yes, sir.

Q. What is their names? (MOG$26MM)

A. Suzy Tiger, Daniel Tiger.

Q. Roman Tiger? (MOG$26MM)

A. Yes, sir. I guess so. And one called Melinda.

Q. Three of them? (MOG$26MM)

A. Yes, sir.

Q. Did you ever hear of an Indian by the name of Timmie Jessie? (MOG$26MM)

A. No.

Q. Nellie Fish? (MOG$26MM)

A. No, sir.

Mr. Rogers: We have certified copies here of testimony taken before the County judge, which I would like to introduce if there are no objections.

Document entry 10622 states Oil and Gas Mining Lease, executed May 1, 1912. The parties of the first part are listed as Nellie Fish, Bunnie Jessie, Willie Jessie, Jeanetta Jessie as heirs of Ullie Eagle. The party of the second part is listed as James A. Chapman who issued $400 for the lease and a guarantee of $20 per year.

Mr. McGee: We object to their introduction.

CHAPTER 9

Kate Barnard was raised by her father because her mother had died when she was an infant. When her father came to the Oklahoma Territory he enrolled her at St. Josephine's Catholic School in the fledgling Oklahoma City. It has been suggested the loss of her mother inspired her to speak up for tribal orphans. It could have been that women were heavily involved in suffrage and reform movements. It was probably because she had a conscience.

Bryan County would have originally been under the protection of the Choctaw Nation's Pushmataha District in Blue County. It would have become Tom Needles County in the Indian state of Sequoyah.

Coal County would have originally been under the protection of the Choctaw Nation's Pushmataha District in Atoka County. It would have become Bixby County in the Indian state of Sequoyah.

Craig County would have originally been under the protection of the Cherokee Nation's Cooweescoowee District. It would have become Cherokee County in the Indian state of Sequoyah.

A Model T Ford car cost $590 in 1915 and in 2015 that car on average would be at least $31,000. In 1915, a gallon of gas was 15¢, and today it is $2.50. In America, car ownership is practically a rite of passage. All of those cars need fuel. In 2021, that $1 would equal $31.50.

BRYAN COUNTY

Asias Willis: $1,900.00. Asias could have bought three cars and filled their tanks. ($59,850)

COAL COUNTY

Emily Leader

CRAIG COUNTY

Hunter Proctor

Jincy Lacey, deceased

Charlotte Proctor

Nancy Christie, deceased

Stillwa Grindstone, deceased

Verly M. Coram

Early Carbin

Claude Catcher

Vura Rattlingourd

Dakie Proctor

Gertie Brown

Freddie McCoy

Jake Fair

William Ellick

Benjamin Ellick

Jesse Pogue

Susan Daugherty

Ollie Riley

Earnest Whitmire

Anna Thompson

Margaret Dick

Louie E. L. Wickliffe

Raymond Gibson

Millie Proctor

Tuxie Galcatcher

William Conner: $364.49 ($11,481)

Bertha Capstain: $364.49 ($11,481)

Lucy Conner: $364.49 ($11,481)

Elizabeth Davis

Ida Davis

Bert Davis and Anna Davis $1,600.00 ($50,400)

David Stealer

Mamie Johnson

Carrie Johnson

Julia Johnson

Reuben Johnson

Lewis Johnson

Peter McKinley Johnson

Anna Johnson

Eva Johnson $482.00 ($15,183)

CHAPTER 10

Eben arrives back at Nashoba with a feeling of dread. The next morning, he awakens, wanting to flee like Lot. The same oppressive wind blows and erodes justice as before during the allotment. Eben unknowingly stands before a deluge of greed that propels the gilded age. He intimately experiences a flood of avarice that will sweep away humanity, dignity, and, ultimately, sanity. Tribal peoples being told, in effect, "sink or swim," while the Christian rich occupy indun canoes, the rising tide raising all boats, the birth of Republican optimism becoming a mantra of trickle-down economics.

"What's wrong?"

"I don't know what to do, Exie."

Eben, swimming in despair, has dreaded bringing bad news home to his spouse. She needs no more ill winds. She isn't fragile, just fatigued from her own life. An accurate description of Exia Wade, now Baker, is that she is a lovely lady of thirty. She left her first man because of his abusive nature, departing with two boys and multiple scars. She selected Eben precisely because of his demeanor and the description of his personality by his aunts. His humor and easy ways were accented during the familial sales pitch by his aunties. The fact that Exia found him cute was gravy. Of course, no man is ever what he seems, and Exia has, in their three years of marriage, not adjusted to his lack of nurture toward her children. Sons who need a father now deprived twice. But, she understands his need to set things right and has learned to love him despite his lack of emotion.

"Things didn't go well?" She begins another approach, gleaning for more information.

"He's a snake! I should chop off his head and bury it to save more people from his bite. He will suck the eggs and kill the roost before he is done." Eben says this almost matter-of-factly, which of course, without any point of reference, confuses Exia. She waits for him to declare who and why and finally asks.

"Are you talking about that White Man?"

"*Ome* (Affirmative)."

Eben is always fortunate that his spouse is more skilled at communication than he. What's more, he is blessed by the fact that she has the patience and interest to help him find answers that are within him, masked by his overfamiliarity.

"What did he look like?"

"He's as tall as I am, thin face, with deep set eyes. He wears spectacles and he grows his side hair longer to help cover his balding head. His hair is sandy brown and he smirks, making him look like a goat. You can tell he thinks better of himself. He talked to me like I was a black man, not free." Eben looks out the door, swatting flies that enter.

"You've met his kind before and it didn't stop you from standing up to them," Exia reasons with him and then retrieves a bowl to give him some hominy and fried hog meat, a dish called *tanchee laboona*, and *pashofa* by the Chickasaw.

"That was when I was a lawyer in my own country." Eben's face radiates frustration and fly carcasses bounce into the dirt at the front door.

"You told me that the treaties say that this land would be our peoples until the Lord returns, yes?" She hands him a spoon.

"Uh huh."

"Well the fact that those people have forgotten the truth does not mean that the truth has vanished, does it?" Exia moves from the table to retrieve a pinch of salt.

"No, it is still the truth."

"Then whether you are a lawyer recognized by them or not, you are still a lawyer. You told me that a lawyer's duty is to protect, so protect and do good for that baby girl." She moves outside to stir the *banaha* around in the kettle, with its broth rolling gently under her summer arbor.

Eben looks at her for a long time while she uses her wooden paddle to leverage against the sides of the black pot, bringing bottom cornhusk-wrapped Choctaw tamales to trade places with the top ones in a black pot next to the hominy. Tomorrow is fifth Sunday at church. This means she is preparing her contribution to the potluck. The hominy dish will feed the travelers tonight who will camp. Exia is a chorus of movement, well-timed and instinctual. She never says too much to overly anger him and yet enough to stir contemplation. Eben has not been a perfect husband; he has at times been terse and even menacing. Despite their occasional stumble though, they both seem to have started the process of learning the harmony required of two, the ancient rhythm circling the fire.

Eben stands up finally and moves towards a basin to wash his face. While refreshing his mind he notices near the bed his storage chest partially covered by a quilt. Exia has pulled it out of the woodshed.

CHAPTER 11

Among the Muscogee people the titles for the queendoms assumed a European nuance. The Micco, or Leader, became the Town King. Of course he was only the leader because he was the oldest son of the clan mother who is technically a queen. His ambassador or *Opinayv* (*oben ni ya*) was named speaker. His *Tvstvnake* (*tus ta nagee*) became known as First Warrior. Some dialects say Tustanagee and some Tuskegee, and thus Tuskegee was a queendom that means "warrior." When the Muscogee people were called the Creek Nation they formed their legislature into the House of Kings and House of Warriors, which looks very patriarchal, and in some case because of Christianity it became so. The ancient confederacy would have been men who ruled at the discretion of their mothers. Power was shared, therefore, across the queendoms. Even after some of them became followers of Christianity, they often named their churches for the ceremonial ground some of their relatives still attended. Tuskegee probably lost their medicine maker and so members had to join other grounds that shared the same fire. This is how tribal members know other Creeks across the Muscogee Nation. If your ceremonial fire does not exist then you can share in the fire of a sister fire or mother fire.

The queendoms even refer to each other in matrilineal terms. *Tucabatchee* is a "mother town," or rather, "the mother fire." Tucabatchee members reside predominately in the Wewoka district; in fact a large number are in Holdenville. Kialegee is a daughter town of the Tucabatchee. Kialegee members reside largely around Wetumka. Hutchechubba is a daughter town of the Kialegee. The relationships of the towns are therefore thought of as relatives. The relationships get even more complicated with the clans. Each queendom has multiple clans associated with their animal kindred. If you are Raccoon you cannot marry another Raccoon, even if they are from a daughter town or cousin town. A Raccoon can marry Squirrel or Bear in their own town as long as there is no connection. Unlike the royals of Europe, where incest was the best, the tribes in America like the trees to not come from the same branch.

Oil companies in the boom years tended to be family affairs. Bermont Oil Company was owned by B. B. Jones and his brother Montfort Jones. Perhaps Bermont became B. B., who was an early wildcatter in the Cushing Oil Field. Some of the Cushing field was originally in Okmulgee District of the Muscogee Nation. Had the Indian state of Sequoyah been formed, those Muscogee people would have lived in Tulladega County. Tulladega as a queendom means "head town." Montfort Jones was also the owner of a Bank in Bristow. Levi Jones, L.W., who is the notary for the court, also enjoys the occupation of being a court-appointed guardian for the Ullie claimant Hepsie Mitchell.

Susie Tiger, called as a witness, being first duly sworn on oath by L.W. Jones, Notary Public, in and for Creek County, Oklahoma, testified as follows: Testified without interpreter.

Examination by Mr. Rogers (McMan Oil & Gas, i.e., Chapman-McFarlin)

Q. Your name is Susie Tiger? (MOG$26MM)

A. Yes, sir.

Q. Where do you live? (MOG$26MM)

A. Here.

Q. You are enrolled as a Creek Citizen, are you? (MOG$26MM)

A. Yes, sir.

Q. Do you know Winney Tiger? (MOG$26MM)

A. Yes, sir.

Q. What relation are you? (MOG$26MM)

A. My mother.

Q. When did she die? (MOG$26MM)

A. In 1902, I think. (Year of the Dead Indian Act)

Q. What time? (MOG$26MM)

A. January 5.

Q. What year? (MOG$26MM)

A. 1902.

Ullie's allotment was not in the Edna area or anywhere near Tuskegee Church. It was common practice for Tams Bixby's agents to give allotments of parents across counties. It was thought if the allotments were allowed to be touching, the Indians would retain their tribalism. Individual land meant separate land. Ullie's allotment was in far northwest Creek County. Ullie Eagle was the Cushing Field. Ullie's aunt dies in 1902. Ullie is found hanged in June 1902, nowhere near her allotment. The family seems to have had a run of bad luck. On May 27, 1902, (32 Stat. 245) Congress passed what is euphemistically called the "Dead Indian Act." Ullie is found hanged so close to the passage of the Dead Indian Act, she becomes perhaps it's terrible mascot. In the land records the first non-Indian listed as executing any instrument is by A. H. Purdy, signing with Katie Bear. Purdy himself would be the subject of contested oil leases in the Oklahoma Supreme Court as early as 1923.

Q. Where did she die? (MOG$26MM)

A. Tuskegee.

Q. Was she sister of David Eagle? (MOG$26MM)

A. Yes, sir.

Q. Have you any brothers or sisters? (MOG$26MM)

A. Yes, sir.

Q. What are their names? (MOG$26MM)

A. Roman Tiger and Melinda Tiger.

Q. You have the exact date of the death of your mother? (MOG$26MM)

A. (Indicates by nod of head) Yes, sir. In a Bible.

Q. Where's the Bible? (MOG$26MM)

A. Down home.

Q. Was that record made at the time that she died? (MOG$26MM)

A. Yes, sir.

Q. Do you know Toochie? (MOG$26MM)

A. While not very well. I was little when she died.

Q. Do you know Ullie Eagle? (MOG$26MM)

A. Yes, sir, I remember seeing her.

Q. Who died first: Toochie or Ullie Eagle? Do you remember? (MOG$26MM)

A. Mother did.

Q. Your remember Toochie's Brother Timmy Jesse? (MOG$26MM)

A. I don't remember.

Q. Do you know Nellie Fish? (MOG$26MM)

A. No, sir.

Mr. McGee. Do you know when Ullie Eagle died? (HOG$26MM)

A. No, I forgot.

Q. Do you remember whether it was before or after your mother died? (HOG$26MM)

A. I don't remember.

Q. Who was your mother's mother? (HOG$26MM)

A. I don't know.

Q. You remember your mother's father's name? (HOG$26MM)

A. I don't know.

Mr. Walkup. Do you know whether Toochie had any brothers or sisters or not? (BIA)

A. No, sir, I don't know anything about it.

Q. What is your father's name? (BIA)

A. Pufney Tiger.

Q. He is enrolled as Pufney Tiger? (BIA)

A. Yes, sir.

Q. You don't know anything about the mother of Toochie, do you? (BIA)

A. No, sir.

Q. Do you know Katie Bear? (BIA)

A. I'm just acquainted with her a little bit. They told me Toochie was a sister of Ullie Eagle's mother, and sometimes they say it was her aunt, so I don't know how it is.

Q. Did you know Nellie Fish? (BIA)

A. No, sir.

Mr. McGee. Is this Bible that bears this date now in your possession? (HOG$26MM)

A. Yes, sir.

Q. How long has it been in your possession? (HOG$26MM)

A. Belongs to me, I put it there.

Mr. Rogers. Have you had this Bible in your possession ever since the date of your mother's death? (MOG$26MM)

A. Yes, sir.

Q. You had the Bible ever since? (MOG$26MM)

A. Yes, sir.

Q. And did you make it at the date of death? (MOG$26MM)

A. No, sir, but my sister had it.

Q. You had it since 1903, and your mother died in 1902? (MOG$26MM)

A. My sister had it and I got it from her. She had it in a little book.

Q. The entry was made in 1903? (MOG$26MM)

A. Yes, sir.

Mr. Walkup. It was agreed between counsel that examination may be made of the entry referred to in the Bible in possession of Susie Tiger and a record of entry therein referring to the death of Winney Tiger be made a part of the record in this case. (BIA)

Witness Susie Tiger excused in order to secure the Bible referred to.

J. E. Thrift, called as a witness, being first duly sworn on oath, by L.W. Jones, Notary Public, in and for Creek County, Oklahoma, testified as follows:

Examination by Mr. Rogers (McMan Oil & Gas, i.e., Chapman-McFarlin)

Q. Your name is J. E. Thrift? (MOG$26MM)

A. Yes, sir.

Q. You're a lawyer, are you? (MOG$26MM)

A. I am.

Q. Do you know Katie Bear? (MOG$26MM)

A. I do.

Q. I will ask you if Katie Bear ever came to you and talked to you of the heirship of Ullie Eagle. (MOG$26MM)

A. She did.

Q. He made a diagram from her statement showing the relationship etc.? (MOG$26MM)

A. I could not state at the time I made a diagram purely from her statement. I did make a diagram which was predicated upon her, in the first place, upon a statement made to me by a party by the name of Hicks, I believe. The fact of the business in the diagram is predicated on her testimony, but my understanding of the heirship as shown in the diagram is predicated upon her testimony, as well as statement made by Hicks.

Q. Now in the diagram which purports to show the relationship, I will ask you if the diagram shows the facts as Katie Bear represented them to you, if you remember. (MOG$26MM)

Mr. McGee: Object to that unless it is confined to Katie Bear.

Q. Do you remember any particular statement made to you about Nellie Fish being an heir as shown on the diagram? (MOG$26MM)

A. I cannot say that I can recall any detail or any statement made by her with reference to Nellie Fish. The fact of the business is

I talked with her for some time in my office. I am not sure who the interpreter was. Katie Bear was present at the time. I think H. G. Carruthers was present at the time. We were talking with her with reference to Celia's allotment and her relationship.

Q. That diagram was prepared about that time, was it Mr. Thrift? (MOG$26MM)

A. I could not say whether this diagram was prepared on that occasion or after that time. The fact of it is I talked with the man by the name of Hicks about the same matter.

Q. Who is Hicks? (MOG$26MM)

A. A white man. I don't know whether I made the diagram from his statement or talked with Katie Bear afterwards, or whether I made the diagram in part from Katie's statement and talked with him afterwards.

Q. You don't recall whether at the time you talk with Katie Bear talked with him? (MOG$26MM)

A. If I had talked with Hicks prior to my time with Katie Bear, the matter would have been discussed, but I can't say that I've talked with Hicks prior to that time.

Susie Tiger recalled as a witness

Mr. Rogers. Can you turn at that place, Susie, for us? (MOG$26MM)

Witness opens Bible and turns to page and states "Here it is."

Q. Is that January 5, 1902? (MOG$26MM)

A. Yes, sir, I think it is.

Q. The Bible shows January 5, 1902. (MOG$26MM)

Mr. Walkup (BIA): The Bible in possession of Susie Tiger, and entry appears therein as follows: "Pufney Tiger died in the summer of 1900, July 31, aged 45 years. Winey, his wife died January 5, 1902, aged 42 years."

Mr. Walkup (BIA): It is agreed between counsels that this hearing is continued to Okmulgee, Tuesday July 8, 1913, at 10 o'clock, at T. J. Farrar's office.

CHAPTER 12

In Kate Barnard's third annual report, beginning October 1, 1910 to October 1, 1911, she notes that the Assistant Attorney General of the United States relayed to her a situation regarding a Muscogee child who was nine years old. The quotes states;

"A guardian has been appointed for his person and property, but nothing appears to have been done for the benefit of the ward, the child living in a hovel situated on an alley adjoining the livers stable with some of his relatives. He is not in school and is not properly clothed, while his estate is claimed by his guardian to be worth in the neighborhood of $3,000, according to the file in the office of the County Court."

Kate issued the quote before noting that one of her case workers, Hobard Huson, came upon "three children in one of the counties of this State, living in the woods like animals, without clothing upon them, who once in a while would go into the nearest village and beg or steal from the inhabitants, which children, upon an investigation, have been found to have valuable property and moneys in the hands of their guardian, that there were being used by the guardian under the legal fiction for the benefit of the children, while actually the children were in the above condition, and the guardian fattening upon their wealth, while the children were growing up in savagery, poverty and crime."

Creek County would have originally been under the protection of the Muscogee Nation's Okmulgee District. It would have become Tulladega County in the Indian state of Sequoyah.

Garvin County would have originally been under the protection of the Chickasaw Nation's Pickens County. It would have become Garvin & McLish counties in the Indian state of Sequoyah.

Grady County would have originally been under the protection of the Chickasaw Nation's Pontotoc County. It would have become Curtis and Bonaparte counties in the Indian state of Sequoyah.

Sallie Scott, a Muscogee girl, was owed $3,000.00. In 1915, a woman could make up to $6 a week, or $312 a year, and buy lunch for 15¢ or as little as 6¢. Sallie was worth nine women working in a year. Irene Cash, a Chickasaw gir was owed $26,000.00. In 1915, Irene had as much funds owed to her as eighty-three women could earn. Food cost went from $1 in 1910 to $66.86 by 2021.

CREEK COUNTY

Sallie Scott: $3,000.00 ($200,580)

Nettie Harjo

GARVIN COUNTY

Sallie Courtney

Willie Courtney

Patterson Shi Cash

Tyree Cash

Elsa Fay Cash

Minnie Ruth Cash

Irene Cash: $26,000.00 ($1,738,360)

GRADY COUNTY

Oliver Brooks

Martin Compelube

Annie Pearle Compelube: $5,000.00 ($334,300)

CHAPTER 13

Eben carries the chest down a path about one hundred yards from his home to his family's camphouse. He feels the tension in his back, fully aware that the leather strap handles are making his fingers white. Talk about a table being a Godsend. The table relaxes under a brush arbor that provides dappled shade. The arbor is standard quick assembly: four six-inch posts that are set ten feet by ten feet apart, with the front posts approximately nine feet above grade and the back posts at around seven. Two three-inch posts are set from back to front and lashed with rope. Three three-inch posts are set horizontally across the slant, tied down, and brush is used to cover the expanse. Little has changed in their design from Mississippi but instead of surrounding the ceremonial stomp ground they group around the church, the flame of the Ceremonial fire replaced by the flame of the Holy Spirit. It usually takes no more than half a day for a few of the men to put one up.

Every fifth Sunday, a circuit preacher will visit woodland churches depending on how many churches they serve. Generally a lay speaker or deacon will provide lessons unless a preacher is available for permanent appointment, a very rare privilege. Larger arbors are built to have church during the summer months out in the morning breeze before the noon sun tortures everyone into lethargy. The logic of church arbors relatively involves the logic of "Better to be cool, slapping the flies under the open, than to be inside the church." Interiors of churches in the summer are ovenlike, even with the shutters and doors wide open. Sit long and you will bake in a Choctaw bug casserole.

Eben's family camphouse is right next to the creek. It is early summer and the water skips over the rocks. The sound is as pleasant as the occasional cool breeze off of the creek face that smells like heaven. He pulls up a chair and opens the chest to begin perusing papers, hoping boredom will give him some nap time. Eben squints constantly, having difficulty in remembering what his abbreviations stand for, attempting to discern squiggles from simple illegibility.

The boxes are records of his activities as a Rail Road Inspector and revenue Officer for the Choctaw Nation Treasury. This is before he was exiled into being a clerk for the Attorney Telle. His political skills were not that well honed in his early twenties. He had been a supporter of Jacob Jackson, who carried a stigma as being a rabble-rouser. Jacob Jackson is akin to Chitto Harjo, the Creek Zapata: dark brown, outspoken, and militant. Essentially, Eben is painted with the same complexion, and his two-year career ends upon the election cycle.

Sifting through the chest, Eben marvels at how quickly he learned to mail notices to recalcitrant mineral permit holders. He had been successful in ferreting information from Lighthorsemen who were traveling to Muskogee. Recon data from law officers was and is critical to the game. In addition, he was fortunate to know a few Bureau of Indian Affairs insiders who actually liked Indian people, and gleaned information as to who to serve notices to as well as who was using storefront properties as a diversion. It was a given that 99 percent of the permit holders would try to abscond without making royalty payments. Eben loved tracking them.

These mineral lessors, through their maneuvers, played with the Choctaw revenue officers like babes in a crib. The babes attempted to enforce laws through wooden bars. The 1866 treaty had gutted the Choctaw Nation of its ability to eject illegal aliens, so these lessors would not pay the permit fees, failed to declare the tonnage of coal they shipped out of the nation, and flat-out lied about it.

Eben swam through lengthy correspondences from these lessors who employed fleets of clerks to write responses. The clerks used language like pirates and flew multiple colors to confuse. These mineral companies' incestuous affairs with the railroads made them more privateer than pirate because it was done under a sanctioned legality. Eben found himself moored without a sail, demanding payment for the Choctaw Nation without authority to force collection. The U.S. legislatively made the Choctaw use wet powder in their cannons. If the railroads would declare the tonnage shipped it would have been easy to collect, but the rail companies had statehood on their mind so they could have government they could control.

Eben digs for three hours under the arbor, gleaning through mounds of notes in the chest, notes on who individuals were, notices he had mailed to federal marshals, notes on correspondence to the Choctaw Attorney

General, notes mostly chronological but cryptically distorted by memory. Whom was he tracking? What was the outcome?

One note involved his notice to the federal marshals about intercepting the payroll shipments on the stage route at Scullyville from D. Kirk, a coal magnate wannabee who had not paid a cent on tons of coal. D. Kirk is Daniel Kirk, and his notation is followed by names of others who were listed on the "ine-Oak Coal Company as shareholders, all scribbled on Eben's wrinkled papers. To anyone but Eben the writings would look like the Rosetta stone flecked with American-looking names protruding from Choctaw sentences.

Eben's literacy is beginning to numb from fighting the egg-and-sausage-induced brain fog and he nods. He resorts to reading the names out loud to remain focused: "T. Jenkins, J. Colbert, J. Blaine, G. McFarland," and then one name turns slightly sideways, with just a "W" and an "S," followed by a barely legible elongated squiggle. He stares intently at this listing and then mouths "William Skinner."

Upon reading the name Eben pulls a blank piece of paper and begins writing, "Dear Ms. Barnard. . . ."

CHAPTER 14

"Oklahoma" was coined by the Choctaw Chief, the Presbyterian Reverend Allen Wright. It translates Okla- for "people" and -homa for "red"—Red People. It was the name of the state given in reluctance to the loss of the statehood for Sequoyah, the last stand legally before the new white laws were thrust upon the tribes of Oklahoma. When Oklahoma was a territory in 1893, a full year before the rollout of the Curtis Act, it was already notorious as the divorce capitol of the United States, where any resident could divorce anyone after ninety days of residency. The leaders of the tribes had been prescient, knowing that with white men come white laws and divorce from property rights would soon arrive. Marriage covenants were remarkably like treaties in the new state—some covenants were easily laid aside. By the close of 1907, in the first year of Oklahoma, 4,366 oil and gas leases were executed on tribal citizens' properties and oilmen had new wives.

Ida Tarbell had written her book in 1904 about the history of Standard Oil and the ruthlessness of John D. Rockefeller. She wrote that he had told a refiner who did not want to sell to him that "the coal oil business belongs to us," meaning Standard Oil. Indeed Rockefeller had control of rail lines, pipelines, storage depots, and refineries across the nation. Rockefeller had his eye on Tulsa. He openly bragged that he owned people in the Department of Interior because he didn't like negotiating with the tribal nations. It was railroads, after all, that had financed the Boomer David Payne's invasion of the Cherokee Strip, leading to the land run of 1889. In the memorial for the state of Sequoyah, Alexander Posey, a Muscogee citizen and secretary of the convention, wrote, "The joint statehood propaganda has been engineered and dominated by the attorneys of the railroads of Indian Territory. The National Committeeman of the Democratic Party is an attorney for the M. K. & T. Railroad, and the National Committeeman of the Republican Party is an attorney for the Frisco Railroad. In case of a joint

State, the railroad attorneys would exercise a dominant influence, and we have cause to fear that a joint State would not properly protect the interests of our people in these suits with the railroads."

Ohio is where Rockefeller controlled the world. Rockefeller was king. Ohio was already under the spell of political kingmaker Mark Hanna as well. Hanna had successfully gotten William McKinley elected, and thus Teddy Roosevelt. Hanna and Rockefeller were old high school classmates. Hanna had successfully blocked the populist William Jennings Bryan, who would become the cowardly lion in Baum's book of Oz. There were no election laws about campaign finance in the 1890s, and so Rockefeller owned more than a few congressmen. It was Congress who designed the Dawes Commission. It was Congress who turned down the state of Sequoyah even though it had been voted on by Indians and Whites on November 7, 1905, where among 65,352 voting citizens, 9,073 voted against the adoption, and 56,279 voted in favor of the adoption of the Constitution. A popular ballot does not always work. Strangely, the Delaware and the Cherokee had been guaranteed representation in the House of Representatives by treaty, a provision that was never enforced.

In the new state of Oklahoma, the Ohio-born Charles Haskell was elected on a platform of reform. He was clear that Ohio-born Rockefeller would not get a pipeline into the Oklahoma oil field. A few years later, Teddy Roosevelt commented to the magazine *Outlook* that it was odd that Governor Haskell owned shares in a company named Prairie Oil and Gas. Prairie Oil, it seems, was allowed to build a pipeline into Tulsa. Prairie Oil also bought out the Bermont Oil Co., and thus large amounts of the Cushing field. The Jones brothers could now keep up with the Jones after the buyout. Prairie Oil was a subsidiary of Standard Oil and the pipeline was to the Neodesha Kansas Refinery owned by Standard Oil and thus by Ohio-born Rockefeller.

Sampson Scott, being first duly sworn by Thomas J. Farrar, A Notary Public, and examined through Dave Grayson, official Creek Interpreter, testified as follows:

Direct Examination by Mr. Rogers:

Q. What is your name? (MOG$26MM)

A. Sampson Scott.

Q. How old are you? (MOG$26MM)

A. Forty-two.

Q. Where do you live? (MOG$26MM)

A.Wetumka. North seven miles.

Q. Are you a Creek Citizen? (MOG$26MM)

A. Yes.

Q. Did you know Ullie Eagle in her lifetime? (MOG$26MM)

A. Yes.

Q. Where did she live, if you know? (MOG$26MM)

A. In Artussee Town.

Q. Is that northwest of Okmulgee? (MOG$26MM)

A. Northwest.

Q. Is Ullie Eagle dead? (MOG$26MM)

A. Yes.

Q. Do you know when she died? (MOG$26MM)

A. She died June 8, 1902.

Q. What caused her to die, if you know? (MOG$26MM)

A. She was hung by a rope to a tree. Don't know who did the work.

Q. Was anybody else hanged at the same time, if you know? (MOG$26MM)

A. Hannah was with her and they were both hung.

Q. Hannah who? (MOG$26MM)

A. Her first name was Hannah Scott, or Bear.

Q. Was Hannah Bear related to you in any way? (MOG$26MM)

A. She is related to me.

Q. Were you present at the funeral? (MOG$26MM)

A. Yes.

Q. Who was Ullie Eagle's mother? (MOG$26MM)

A. Toochie.

Q. Who was the father of Ullie Eagle, if you know? (MOG$26MM)

A. Dave Eagle.

Q. Is Toochie living or dead? (MOG$26MM)

A. Dead.

Q. Did she die before or after Ullie Eagle died? (MOG$26MM)

A. Toochie died first.

Q. Is Dave Eagle living or dead? (MOG$26MM)

A. Dead.

Q. Did he die before after Ullie Eagle died? (MOG$26MM)

A. Dave died first.

Q. Did Dave Eagle leave any brothers or sisters, if you know? (MOG$26MM)

A. Winney Tiger, a sister.

Q. Is she living or dead? (MOG$26MM)

A. Dead.

Q. Did Toochie leave any brothers or sisters, if you know? (MOG$26MM)

A. A sister, Nellie.

Q. Nellie Fish? (MOG$26MM)

A. Yes.

Q. Is she living or dead? (MOG$26MM)

A. Living or dead?

Q. Where is she living? (MOG$26MM)

A. East of Wetumka.

Q. She married or single? (MOG$26MM)

A. Married.

Q. Who is her husband? (MOG$26MM)

A. Willy Fish.

Entry 12806 in Creek County notes a Deed executed by Nellie Fish and Weleya Fish in the first part and William P. Morton in the second part for a consideration of $50. On September 18, 1914 with the thumbprints of Nellie and Weleya. In a later Oklahoma Supreme Court case it was upheld that "Riley Cleveland, Willie Perkins, William P. Morton, and John F. Hayden entered into a conspiracy to defraud the plaintiff out of his land, and that the deeds under which defendants claim were procured under false and fraudulent representations and conduct of said parties." The Court went onto say, "The finding of the trial court as to the fraudulent transaction of Cleveland and Morton are amply supported by the evidence."

Q. Did Toochie have a brother, if you know? (MOG$26MM)

A. Yes.

Q. What was his name? (MOG$26MM)

A. Timmie Jesse.

Q. Is he living or dead? (MOG$26MM)

A. Dead.

Q. Did he leave a wife, or do you know? (MOG$26MM)

A. A wife, yes.

Q. What is her name? (MOG$26MM)

A. Eliza.

Q. What is her name now? (MOG$26MM)

A. Eliza Spaniard.

Q. Did Timmie Jesse leave any children? (MOG$26MM)

A. Yes.

Q. Did you know their names? (MOG$26MM)

A. No, sir.

Q. Who was Toochie's father? (MOG$26MM)

A. Suntullo Fixico.

Suntullo Fixico is listed as Santala on census card 2614. Santala is listed as being deceased from Artussee. Santala was married to Liddy who is listed as being deceased and from Kialegee. Kialegee is a modern spelling of the Muscogee word *Ekvlace* (*Egah-laygee*) which means "head left." This queendom left a calling card when they went to war. They cut the heads off of their enemy and stacked them. The Kialegee are the daughter town of the Tucabatchee. An old Hank Williams song mispronounced the name Kawliga. When Swanton came among the Muscogee for the Department of Ethnology at the Smithsonian, he noted that the Tucabatchee and Kialegee ceremonial grounds had small mounds built there. The two conservative queendoms had brought their ancient culture of mound-building with them.

Q. Was Suntollo Fixico the father of Nellie Fish? (MOG$26MM)

A. I heard he was the father.

Mr. McGee. I object to that and ask that that answer be stricken from the record.

Mr. Rogers. Was Suntollo Fixico the father of Timmie Jesse? (MOG$26MM)

A. Yes, sir.

Q. I'll ask you to state if it was the generally concerned and regarded by the Indians who knew Nellie Fish and Timmie Jesse, if they were known to be brother and sister. (MOG$26MM)

A. Yes.

Q. How far does Nellie Fish live from you now? (MOG$26MM)

Nellie Fish on census card 2614 is listed as Kialegee, the matrilineal descent from Liddy. Even though her father was Artussee, she followed her mother, as is traditional. Nellie is married to Weleya Fish, who is from the queendom of Alabama. The Alabama Quassarte are in Oklahoma and the Alabama Coushatta are in Texas. The Alabama language is a bridge language between Muscogee and Choctaw. The Alabama ceremonial grounds continue to this day. It is oral history that the ceremonial grounds carried the hot coals from their ceremonial grounds in Alabama, never allowing the ancient ceremonial fire to extinguish. The coals were carried by holy men of the grounds in a pot suspended by being lashed to two poles carried by the four men. The fire, carried like the Ark of the Covenant, guaranteed that the Alabama people would not perish from the earth.

A. He doesn't know how far, about ten miles.

Q. Did you formally live in Artussee town, out west of Okmulgee? (MOG$26MM)

A. Yes, sir. That is where he used to live.

Q. How long have you lived down about Wetumka? (MOG$26MM)

A. Been living at Wetumka some time.

Q. Several years? (MOG$26MM)

A. Yes. (MOG$26MM)

Q. About how many years?

A. Been living there some time. Don't know how long.

Q. You knew Timmie Jesse in his lifetime? (MOG$26MM)

A. Yes, sir.

Q. Do you know Katie Bear? (MOG$26MM)

A. Yes.

Q. Where does she live? (MOG$26MM)

A. She is living in Argosy (Artussee) town.

Q. How far does she live from where Ullie Eagle was killed or hung? (MOG$26MM)

A. About a mile and a half.

Cross-examination by Mr. McGee.

Q. Where were you living at the time Ullie Eagle died? (HOG$26MM)

A. At Wetumka.

Q. Were you present at the burial of Ullie Eagle? (HOG$26MM)

A. No, sir, he was not present. He was there the next day, but he was present when Hannah Scott was buried.

Q. How do you know Ullie Eagle died on June 8, 1902? (HOG$26MM)

A. He said he looked at the records of the books. He saw it.

Q. What book is it that has the records? (HOG$26MM)

A. He seen it at Hannah Scott's father, he has a book on it and he has a book of it to.

Q. Does this book tell when Ullie Eagle died? (HOG$26MM)

A. Yes.

Q. Where does Hannah Scott's father live? (HOG$26MM)

A. He is dead. Used to live out here in Argosy.

Q. Who has that book now? (HOG$26MM)

A. He has got it (meaning the witness).

Q. How long have you had this book? (HOG$26MM)

A. He has had it for a long time, he has got it at home.

Q. Who did you say Toochie's father was? (HOG$26MM)

A. Suntullo Fixico.

Q. Who was her mother? (HOG$26MM)

A. Don't know Toochie's mother.

Q. Did you know Suntullo Fixico? (HOG$26MM)

A. I don't know him.

Q. Did you ever know him? (HOG$26MM)

A. I don't know.

Q. How do you know Suntullo Fixico is the father of Toochie? (HOG$26MM)

A. I was told by some people that he was father.

Q. Who told you he was the father? (HOG$26MM)

A. No one told him but he heard it that he was the father.

Q. When did you hear it? (HOG$26MM)

A. I couldn't tell when it was. Don't know.

Q. Who was Timmie Jesse's father? (HOG$26MM)

A. Suntullo Fixico.

Q. Who was Timmie Jesse's mother? (HOG$26MM)

A. I don't know.

Q. Who was Timmie Jesse's brother? (HOG$26MM)

A. I don't know.

Q. How do you know that Suntullo Fixico was his father? (HOG$26MM)

A. I heard people talking of him as his father.

Q. When did you hear that? (HOG$26MM)

A. He don't remember.

Q. Did you ever hear anybody say who his mother was? Timmie Jesse's mother? (HOG$26MM)

A. I never heard.

Q. They told you who his father was, but never told you who his mother was? (HOG$26MM)

A. No, sir.

Q. How long have you know Timmie Jessie? (HOG$26MM)

A. I know him for some time.

Q. When did you see him last? (HOG$26MM)

A. Last time I seen him they were having a ball game about ten years ago, maybe more.

Stickball among the five tribes is played with two sticks and the Muscogee called their sticks *da-hon-i-gee*. The northern tribes play with one stick. Since the sticks are made by bending the wood at the top it is suggested that is why it was called La Crossier by the French. Why it is now called Lacrosse is a happy accident.

Q. When did Timmie Jessie die? (HOG$26MM)

A. I don't know.

Q. Do you know who raised Timmie Jessie? (HOG$26MM)

A. I don't know.

Q. Did you ever see him with Suntullo Fixico? (HOG$26MM)

A. No, sir.

Q. All you know about him is that Suntullo Fixico is his father, is that it? (HOG$26MM)

A. Yes, sir.

Q. That is all that you ever heard about him? (HOG$26MM)

A. Yes, sir.

Q. How long have you known Nellie Fish? (HOG$26MM)

A. For some time.

Q. Who was Nellie Fish's father? (HOG$26MM)

A. Suntullo Fixico.

Q. Who was Nellie Fish's mother? (HOG$26MM)

A. I don't know the name of the mother.

Q. How do you know that Suntullo Fixico is her father? (HOG$26MM)

A. I heard it.

Q. Who told you? (HOG$26MM)

A. Just heard parties talking about it.

Q. Can't you remember who told you that? (HOG$26MM)

A. No, sir.

Q. Did you ever see Nellie Fish with Suntullo Fixico? (HOG$26MM)

A. No. sir.

Q. Do you know whether Suntullo Fixico and Nellie Fish's mother ever lived together or not? (HOG$26MM)

A. No, sir.

Q. Who raised Nellie Fish? (HOG$26MM)

A. Her mother.

Q. Did you ever see her with her mother? (HOG$26MM)

A. No, sir.

Q. Where did her mother live? (HOG$26MM)

A. Living east of Wetumka.

Q. Did you ever see Timmie Jessie and Nellie Fish together? (HOG$26MM)

A. No, sir.

Q. Did you ever see Timmie Jessie with his mother? (HOG$26MM)

A. No, sir.

Q. You say you can't remember when Timmie Jessie died? (HOG$26MM)

A. I don't know.

Q. Isn't it a fact that you don't know whether or not Suntullo Fixico is the father of Nellie Fish? (HOG$26MM)

A. Suntullo Fixico is the father of Nellie Fish.

Q. Who told you that? (HOG$26MM)

A. I heard parties telling that he was her father.

Q. Who was the parties you heard telling that? (HOG$26MM)

A. No one didn't tell him.

Q. When was the first time that you heard who Nellie Fish's father was? (HOG$26MM)

A. Said he couldn't remember when it was, said he heard parties telling about it, said he can't set the date.

Q. Did you ever hear more than one party say that? (HOG$26MM)

A. Just heard about it from people talking about it.

Q. How many people did you hear say that? (HOG$26MM)

A. Several people.

Q. How many? (HOG$26MM)

A. He don't know.

Q. Fifty? (HOG$26MM)

A. He don't know.

Q. You testified that it was the general opinion in the community that Suntullo Fixico was the father of Timmie Jessie; how many people did you hear say that? (HOG$26MM)

A. He don't know, don't remember the people that said that.

Q. Where was it that you heard this? (HOG$26MM)

A. He don't remember.

Q. What general community? (HOG$26MM)

A. He don't remember, he says, he never have gone outside of the Indian Territory.

Q. It was somewhere in Indian Territory, wasn't it? (HOG$26MM)

A. Yes.

Q. How old was Timmie Jessie when he died? (HOG$26MM)

A. He don't know.

Q. Do you know about how old he was? (HOG$26MM)

A. He don't know.

Q. Did Timmie Jessie and Nellie Fish have the same mother? (HOG$26MM)

A. Different mothers.

Q. Who was Nellie Fish's mother? (HOG$26MM)

A. I don't know her mother.

Q. How do you know they had different mothers? (HOG$26MM)

A. I hear it was different mothers, some parties told me.

Q. Isn't it a fact that you have also heard that Nellie Fish's father and mother never did live together as husband and wife? (HOG$26MM)

A. I don't know whether they lived together or not.

Q. Did you ever see Nellie Fish and her father and mother together? (HOG$26MM)

A. No, sir.

Q. Did you ever see her mother and father together a single time? (HOG$26MM)

A. No, sir.

Q. All you know about it is that Suntullo Fixico is the father of Nellie Fish and Timmie Jessie? (HOG$26MM)

A. That is all he knows, he says.

RE-DIRECT EXAMINATION BY MR. ROGERS

Q. Were you raised in Artussee town? (MOG$26MM)

A. I was born in Artussee Town.

Q. Did the Indians living around there prior to the date Ullie Eagle died generally understand that Suntullo Fixico was the father of Toochie and Nellie and Timmie? (MOG$26MM)

A. Yes.

Q. What kin are you to Tullamarsee Scott? (MOG$26MM)

A. He's my father.

Q. Your father? (MOG$26MM)

A. Yes.

Q. You know Katie Bear? (MOG$26MM)

A. Yes.

Q. And those old Indians always knew that Suntullo Fixico was the father of these three? (MOG$26MM)

Instrument 13467 was executed in Creek County on October 8, 1914. It is a Quit Claim Deed executed in the 1st part by Nellie Fish and in the 2nd part by James A. Chapman (McMan Oil & Gas, i.e., Chapman-McFarlin) and Montfort Jones. Quit Claim deeds relinquish all rights. The Order of Approval indicates something disturbing: "The said petitioner appearing in person and by her attorney of record, O.A. Morton, and it being made to appeal to the court that the petitioner (Nellie Fish) is a resident of Hughes County, Oklahoma, and to be required to appear in this court at a later date would necessitate an extra trip and additional expense to the said petitioner (Nellie Fish), and there being no good reason why her testimony could not be taken and should not be taken while she is present in court on the 8th day of October, 1914, and the Honorable Natt Ligon, and F. L. Montgomery, United States probate attorneys in and for Creek County, Oklahom being present."

Q. I will ask you to state what the people generally said up there in that vicinity about the relationship between Suntullo Fixico, Toochie, Nellie and Timmie. (MOG$26MM)

A. I heard about the relationship.

Q. What relation? (MOG$26MM)

A. Same father.

Q. Did you hear the same thing from the Indians down around Wetumka? (MOG$26MM)

A. Yes, I heard the same thing.

RE-CROSS EXAMINATION BY MR. MAGEE

Q. Did you ever hear anything said about the mother of Timmie Jessie, Nellie Fish, and Toochie? (HOG$26MM)

A. No, sir.

Q. Never heard anything said about his mother? (HOG$26MM)

A. Never heard about it.

Q. Where was Nellie Fish born? (HOG$26MM)

A. I don't know.

Q. Where does she live now? (HOG$26MM)

A. East of Wetumka.

Q. How long has she lived there? (HOG$26MM)

A. Some time.

Q. How long? (HOG$26MM)

A. I don't know.

Q. Didn't you ever see her? (HOG$26MM)

A. No, sir.

Q. How long since you lived over in Artussee Town? (HOG$26MM)

A. I don't know how long I have lived there. I didn't hardly live there. I go back and forth, don't stay at one place.

Q. Where do you stay the most of the time now? (HOG$26MM)

A. Most of the time I stay in Wetumka. My home is in Wetumka.

Q. How long have you been staying in Wetumk? Most of the time? (HOG$26MM)

A. I don't know how long I stayed there.

Q. Where were you born? (HOG$26MM)

A. Born in Artussee.

Q. How long have you lived there? (HOG$26MM)

A. I don't know.

Q. How old were you when you heard that Nellie Fish, Timmie Jessie, and Toochie had the same father? (HOG$26MM)

A. Don't know how old he was.

Q. Who did you ever talk to about Timmie Jessie, Nellie Fish, and Toochie? (HOG$26MM)

A. Don't remember. Don't know.

Q. Don't you remember anybody you talked to about them? (HOG$26MM)

A. I don't remember.

Q. Didn't you ever talk to Mr. Rogers about them? (HOG$26MM)

A. I remember I talked with Rogers once.

Q. When was the first time you ever talked to Rogers about them? (HOG$26MM)

A. I don't remember when it was.

Q. Did you ever talk to Mr. Scales about them, the gentleman who was sitting in the window a minute ago? (HOG$26MM)

A. Never did talk to Scales.

Q. Didn't you ever talk to Scales about anything? (HOG$26MM)

A. No, sir.

Q. Do you know whether Mr. Scales can talk Creek or not? (HOG$26MM)

A. Yes, he can talk Creek.

Q. How do you know he can talk Creek? (HOG$26MM)

A. I heard him talking Creek.

Q. But he never talked to you? (HOG$26MM)

A. I don't talk with him and he don't talk with me.

BY MR. WALKUP

Q. Did Timmie Jessie die before the death of Ullie Eagle?

A. I don't remember which one died first.

Q. Did Winney Tiger die before or after the death of Ullie Eagle?

A. Ullie died first.

BY MR. McGee

Q. When did Winney Tiger die? (HOG$26MM)

A. I don't know when.

Q. Have you any record of the death of Winney Tiger? (HOG$26MM)

A. Haven't got it.

Q. How do you know Winney Tiger died after Ullie Eagle? (HOG$26MM)

A. When Hannah Scott died she was at the funeral and Winey was there.

Q. There are two Winney Tigers, aren't there? (HOG$26MM)

A. Yes, two.

Q. A Winney Tiger died out here about a month ago, wasn't there? (HOG$26MM)

A. I don't know this Winney Tiger that lived out here.

Q. Do you know that the Winney Tiger that you saw at the time Hannah Scott was buried was the same Winney Tiger that was the sister of Dave Eagle? (HOG$26MM)

A. Yes.

Q. How do you know that? (HOG$26MM)

A. They used to run around together and was acquainted.

Q. Used to run around with Winney Tiger? (HOG$26MM)

A. Yes, and Dave.

What is missing from the case is even more troubling. On May 1, 1912, the Oil and Gas Mineral Lease was secured to James A. Chapman (McMan Oil & Gas, i.e., Chapman-McFarlin) for $400. What is not discussed is the Mortgage of Real Estate done on May 23, 1912. Nellie Fish and Willea Fish execute a mortgage with George L. Mann, Harry H. Rogers (Attorney for McMan Oil & Gas), and Vernon W. Harris of Hughes County. Nellie and Willea were given $800 with a promisory note due January 11, 1913 with interest at 10%. Of course they were expected to insure any buildings against loss by fire and tornado and ensure all property taxes paid. The document is signed by Tim H. Proctor for the x mark made by Nellie Fish and Willea Fish. Nellie was upside down in a loan on property that will be worth $26,000,000. The Fish heirs never saw a dime.

CHAPTER 15

Good Angel Kate was only successful in investigating and prosecuting one-hundred and seven cases in twenty-five counties in Oklahoma. It was herself, Prosecutor Stolper, and one other aide. Early pictures of her displayed a lovely brunette of refinement and optimism, complete with a fine hat. At the end of her life, her pictures appear full of sorrow and despair for her failure to protect children. Her statue now in the bottom of the state capitol does not have the same emotion as her later pictures where her eyes seem shallow, darkened by questions, haunted by the word, "Why?"

Haskell County would have originally been under the protection of the Choctaw Nation's Moshulatubbee District in San Bois County. It would have become San Bois & Thomas counties in the Indian state of Sequoyah.

Hughes County would have originally been under the protection of the Muscogee Nation's Wewoka District. It would have become Spokogee and Cussehta counties in the Indian state of Sequoyah. Kate did not have the resources to investigate the most corrupt counties of Hughes and McCurtain counties. In McCurtain County, Stolper found evidence that someone was forcing Choctaws to sign life insurance policies and then eat ground glass with carbolic acid to collect the proceeds. The Hughes County Holdenville Court house is where Angie Debo noted in *And Still the Waters Run* the greatest level of forgery was taking place in Oklahoma. The judge in this county was so corrupt that John Cordell informed the federal government that "forgery in securing deeds is now the rule instead of the exception." It was recorded by Debo that one Muscogee girl was handed a pencil and then she was given the receipt with an x mark for her Hughes County allotment. Hughes County is the seat of McMan Oil owned by Chapman, McFarlin, and Rogers. One prominent Wetumka oil man, Ray Meadors, was named *Este Baba* by Kialegee elder James Wesley; it means "Man-eater."

In 1915, a family budget for a husband, wife, and three kids was on average, $28 a month for food, $4 for utilities, $1.50 for riding streetcar, $9 for everyone's clothes, and $1 for general household expenses. $43 a month for 5 people to live well, which means the family would cost $516 a year. A single child would cost about $56 to feed in a year. In 1910, an American Indian minor or orphan in Oklahoma with $1 for food could buy $66.86 of food in 2021. In Haskell County, those American Indian minors would be owed over $14,208,591.77 to buy food.

HASKELL COUNTY

John Wallen

Elish Wallen

Reubin Wallen

Absolum Wallen: $1,080.00 ($72,208.80)

Jefferson Davis

Joseph Ed. Coley: $878.51 ($58,737.18)

Sarah Grady Coleman, dec.: $820.00 ($54,825.20)

William H. Cotner: $9,334.87 ($624,129.41)

Henrietta Woods

Esther Woods

Jimmie Woods: $1,265.00 ($84,577.90)

James Ledbetter: $252.00 ($16,848.72)

Bud Ledbetter: $245.50 ($16,414.13)

Julia Ledbetter: $170.43 ($11,394.95)

George Ledbetter: $192.73 ($12,885.93)

Her May King: $2,500.00 ($167,150)

Jackson James: $32,702.00 ($2,186,455.72)

Myrtle Leflore: $220.89 ($14,768.70)

Noel Leflore, dec.: $30,593.00 ($2,045,447.98)

Lula Perry: $325.85 ($21,786.33)

Winnie Stallaby: $95.00 ($6,351.70)

Hattie Stallaby: $154.05 ($10,299.78)

Josephine Forrest: $61.05 ($4,081.80)

Lena V. Forrest: $203.36 ($13,596.64)

Belle Young, dec.: $42,536.00 ($2,843,956.96)

Maggie Cravens: $203.36 ($13,596.65)

Opal Gertrude Holder: $451.66 ($30,197.99)

Willmot Ellnora Holder: $920.35 ($61,534.60)

Edis Imogine Holder: $164.08 ($10,970.39)

Thompson McKinney: $1,127.15 ($75,361.25)

James J. McKinney: $325.00 ($21,729.50)

Annie Mary Jackson: $842.50 ($56,329.55)

Austin McCann, dec.: $500.00 ($33,430)

Lewis Cass: $1,722.00 ($115,132.92)

Mary Ann Stallaby: $310.00 ($20,726.60)

Wilson Thomas: $339.38 ($22,690.95)

Stephen Thomas: $50.00 ($3,343)

Nora Kidwell: $992.36 ($66,349.19)

Charlotte Bascom: $760.56

Lester Luce: $356.00

Elbert Luce: $4,000.00

Herbert Luce: $90.00

Sister Luce: $315.47

Pear Luce: $121.96

Sophie Luce: $91.75

Nora Mason: $1,863.99

Earle Mason: $6,900.00

Simpson Evans

Rufus Evans

Edna Jackson

Amos Mcintosh

Lonna Garland: $627.74

Henry Garland: $779.87

Luke Bond: $1,733.00

Gertrude Holleman: $1,621.09

Wilber Holleman: $2,085.54

Eugene Holleman: $1,904.38

Elish Wallen

John Wallen

Ansolum Wallen

Amos W. Christy: $195.99

Daniel Webster

Julia McCann

Sampson Francis McCann

Elizabeth Perry: $73.66

Laviria Perry: $73.66

Anne Perry: $73.66

Newman Anderson

Levisey Anderson

Minnie Nail

Alex Scott children

Carrie Bell Freeman: $300.00

Arthur C. Freeman: $300.00

Herman E. Smith: $322.33

Ora G. Smith: $322.33

John Tom

Elsie Tom: $259.00

Earle Folsom: $1,040.00

Bennie Walls

Bertha Walls

Herbert Walls: $750.00

Nancy Lauretta Hildebrand: $247.29

Denver Garland: $103.97

Peter Garland: $144.00

Gilbert Marris: $1,040.00

Mary Ellen Quinton: $1,000.00

Leo Perry: $158.34

Walter Allen: $676.94

Willie Grady Stigler

Annie Perry

Levina Perry

Herman E. Smith

Ora G. Smith

Claud R. Smith

Elmer McKinney

Jonas Wade: $1,117.20

Gency Tom: $664.75

Isom Wallen: $107.50

Rose Ann Wallen: $41.56

Mary Barnett: $188.06

Annie A. Barnett: $8.62

Henry Clay Barnett: $12.56

Alexander Barnett, Jr.: $16.91

Minnie Nail: $914.42

West Nail: $872.31

Lyman H. Gage

Austin Albro Cooper

Callie Layne: $1,653.90

Donald Cass: $220.00

Jefferson Cass: $235.00

Norris Cass: $260.00

Willie Grady Stigler: $7,000.00

Daniel Webster

Myrtle Catherine Layne: $190.13

Peter Cass: $494.84

George Israel Mason: $48.90

Allie Layne: $1,500.97

Her May King: $3,000.00

Ollie Mikey: $274.50

James Barnett: $95.00

George Buckley

Jessie Barnett: $32.00

Boyd Turner Woolridge: $59.75

Myrtle Cass: $511.03

Arthur Bascom: $181.50

Josephine Folsom

Henry Williams

John W. Lantz: $1,222.40

Leb May Lantz

Etta V. Lantz

Frank F. Lantz

Alice Lantz

Ophelia Lantz

Essie Wright

Absolum Wallem

Earle Lantz: $208.40

Salina Luce

Bertha Forrest: $922.44

Dovey Raborn: $270.00

Hubert Holder: $948.00

Opal Louisa King: $2,000.00

Mirtle Robinson: $961.96

Green Robinson: $305.00

Stephen Thomas: $121.96

Wilson Thomas: $315.47

Mary Ann Stalliby

Agnes Woolridge: $789.99

Calvin Robinson: $198.70

Minnie Nail

West Nail: $5,000.00

Albert Dempey

Clifton Cass: $410.69

Newton Garland: $4,040.00

Clara Stirling Garland: $6,188.48

David Wright: $500.00

Austin Albro Cooper 5,000.00

Dawie Ophelia Layne: $1,374.16

Nicie E. Layne: $226.87

Elish Wallen

CHAPTER 16

Eben is a true believer in the purpose of the Choctaw Nation Treasury: collecting funds to pay for schools. During his tenure he has discovered efficiency as a strategy to help expedite the paper war. So he does not have any of the treasury staff copy correspondence unless he is certain they are prepared for the ensuing stormy litigation. The Skinner case is unresolved, otherwise he would not have listed it in his notes. Essentially, in his hubris, he assumed he would one day return to the Treasury and resurrect cold cases; political naiveté comes with being twentysomething.

In his first week as a Rail Inspector (Revenue Collector) for the Treasury he had filed a request that the Indian Inspector of the Bureau of Indian Affairs investigate the loss of royalties from a coal lease near McAlester. The amount of interrogatories and quotation of federal case law from the company's attorneys was almost mirrored word for word from the Bureau of Indian Affairs Solicitor office. The paperwork from that misstep inundated the Treasury Department for four months. Eben grew frustrated having to translate from English to Choctaw and back to English for those required legislative reports. The company had even employed a former Indian Commissioner who no doubt probably ended up helping to write the Curtis Act.

Trench experience is always the best. Eben learned how to maneuver so well that now, by the time he writes the letters to company attorneys, he has his ducks in a row. Of the hundreds of letters he writes and numerous cases he has filed on, he retains notes on a dozen or so because they deal with royalties due to friends. Now Annie is caught in a web he has seen before. The 1893 letter he has in his possession reads:

> Dear Mr. Skinner,
>
> The Choctaw Nation is in receipt of correspondence from the Bureau of Indian Affairs Indian Inspector's office. We have

been notified that you are the Attorney of listing for the Pine-Oak Coal Company, headquartered in Wichita, Kansas.

In reviewing the Legal land descriptions for Allottees our inspectors have located tribal property adjacent to that of Tobias Frazier, whom your company has executed a mineral lease with. The tribe routinely monitors property that is subject to Application for removal of restrictions for leasors. The Bureau Land appraiser's file for Mr. Frazier indicated that Application for removal of restrictions occurred nearly a year and half ago after an execution of the lease with the Pine-Oak Coal Company. Mr. Frazier has indicated that he has been living on his wife's allotment north of Talihina, which is essentially across several mountains from his allotment near Red Oak. Mr. Frazier was unaware if there was mining activity on his lease. He also indicated that he has not been receiving any funds derived from that property regarding the lease executed by the Pine-Oak Coal Company and assumed the lease was not being exercised.

In correspondence to and from the Revenue Inspector for the Bureau, we have confirmed that funds derived from that lease have not been paid and the tribe assumed it was dormant. As a result, the Choctaw Treasury has been in contact with the Lease Division of the Bureau to determine the names of stockholders for the Pine-Oak Coal Company, and subsequently the company lists you as the primary legal counsel.

The Choctaw Treasury has made a site visitation of Mr. Frazier's property. The tribe has observed that the mining activity is on his property and crosses property owned by the Choctaw Nation, not surveyed for rail. As a result, in viewing the loading of coal into rail cars, it was determined that the revenue from the tonnage was not being reported to the Bureau of Indian Affairs or the Choctaw Nation. The royalties therefore have gone unreported with no submission of payment.

The Choctaw Nation would appreciate the name of the rail companies that the Pine-Oak Coal Company contracted with for transportation of the coal from the Choctaw Nation so that we may arrive at an approximate tonnage contracted from your company.

Please be at liberty to provide this information at the earliest time available.

Sincerely,

Silas Battiest – Choctaw Nation Treasurer."

Eben had been a fresh graduate of Jones Academy before attending college at Durant in 1892 when he went to work for Mr. Battiest. Battiest is middle-aged, with salt-and-pepper hair topping an athletic frame that sports a pot belly. His round Choctaw face is usually sober, with a hint of slumber hiding behind the eyelids. He cannot speak English very well, but excels as a politician, giving oration that is as illuminating as it is entertaining. Eben is fascinated by Silas and finds himself daily handing the correspondence to Mr. Battiest and then during the course of explaining its contents waits for some morsel of dry humor. Though Battiest's English is limited, he still loves playing the white man's game.

"You say this company has been loading coal and shipping?" Battiest squints, canvassing the letter, searching for words he might know.

"Uh huh, and I bet we don't get any transportation records."

"How many rail cars did the Lighthorse see?"

"I spoke with the Captain and he counted three that were on the spur. What he didn't know was how fast they were loading and if the shipments were for a day or a week. He did count about thirty men during the shift change." Eben stares out the second-floor windows at the little clouds hovering above the Potato hills.

"Were the miners Italian?" Battiest asks clumsily.

Eben considers asking why that is important, but does not."He didn't say, but ol Isom wouldn't know an Irishman named O'Patrick."

"We haven't had a response from Muskogee on the filing against the Red River Mining Company have we? Has the Attorney General Jones gotten off his lazy butt to file the nations response to that last declaration by the Bureau?" Battiest leans back his wooden executive chair, the springs protesting the shift away from the center of gravity.

Eben fights sarcasm when discussing the Red River case. "No, and we are about six months out on that case, which means that the Bureau Solicitor will no doubt request that the court not hear it until they have chewed on it for about another two. Muskogee will no doubt send the case to DC, which will kill at least six weeks."

"I heard that Wilson will be seeking the Attorney General seat on the next election since he hit his term limit in the Senate."

Battiest's habit of musing about seemingly unrelated topics always entertains Eben. Eben loves playing the mind game and throws in some sarcasm, "Is he still mad about his failed run for Moshulatubbee?"

"Worse, his cousin is a deputy Lighthorse over there near Scullyville. I heard he was telling everyone about Jones campaigning for ol Malachi James this last election. Did I ever tell you what we called Malachi back at Armstrong? We called him *Washkubby* (Mangy)" Battiest said, laughing. "If Wilson gets in here he will probably clean house of suspected James friends and set the collection docket back months while he hires his cousins." Battiest said this leaning his head back fighting the temptation brought by summer fatigue

"I think we should still file against the Pine-Oak Company," Eben redirects.

"I know. Micco Smallwood was telling me on his last rail trip from DC he met a Kansas Congressman's family on a complimentary trip provided by the Texas Louisiana Rail. I bet that Rail Company will be on our side in the Red River case. How much of Red River stock do you figure they have?" Battiest is smirking, eyes closed. "Anyways, the Micco found out about the free trip because the kids were wanting to have a picture with a real live Indian Chief. Apparently the wife just went on and on about her family's blessings because of her husband's leadership. Turns out, it's that same Congressman who has been introducing a bunch of statehood resolutions for Oklahoma Territory. The last one called for the abolishment of Indian Territory outright; the same congressman whose brother is the railroad attorney for Texas Louisiana and a few other companies. I told the Micco that if the Choctaw Rail Company wasn't broke maybe we could offer free trips. I voted yes to start that rail company. As if Indians would ever get contracts with white men." Battiest sits back upright, dips his pen in the well and begins signing the letter. "You will be traveling to the site and find out the name of the rail company yourself, won't you?"

Eben quickly responds, "I have a family friend who will put me up at Rock Creek Church."

CHAPTER 17

All of the railroad lobbyists worked for the adoption of the State of Oklahoma. Payne, the original Boomer, was himself, as a promoter of opening Indian lands, arrested for invasion of tribal property by the Hanging Judge Parker and jailed. In the new Territory, the Supreme Court had ruled in favor of every railroad case that came before it. The railroad promotions of free passes for territorial legislators was rebuffed in the Sequoyah Constitution where this type of lobbying was criminalized. The most famous railroad attorney in the territory was Henry Asp, who would champion the new capitol to be located at Guthrie, his home city.

The machinations of railroads and Standard Oil are legendary. When the Glenn Pool was discovered near Tulsa the ensuing black gold rush stampeded the Muscogee Indians. In March of 1911, two orphan boys died from being dynamited in their home. It wasn't until 1915 that the state of Oklahoma passed a law preventing any individuals from sharing in the estate of a victim for whose death or disablement they may have been responsible. The law was delivered to Oklahoma through the north, so to speak. Not Glinda, but someone called the Sweet Angel Kate. In 1911, she delivered her lists of orphan children who were being swindled by their court-appointed guardians. Case by case she began the impossible effort of finding silver slippers for the thousands of Dorothys, and Kate did so without a magic wand. Of the 105 successful cases she prosecuted, one in Tulsa illuminates her filings.

STATE OF OKLAIDMA,)

) SS.

COUNTY OF TULSA.)

IN THE JUVENILE COURT THEREOF.

In the matter of the State in)
the interest of Sarah Ann)
Perryman, a child under sixteen) No. ______.
years of age.)

PETITION

Comes now Kate Barnard, the duly elected, qualified, and acting Commissioner of Charities and Corrections of the State of Oklahoma, by her general attorney, Ross F. Lockridge, and intervenes as NEXT FRIEND in the above-entitled cause and alleges and says:

1. That Sarah Ann Perryman is a minor orphan child under sixteen years of age, to-wit: Eight years old.

2. That she resides in Tulsa County, Oklahoma, and has estate in said county consisting of land and other interests, which is being mismanaged and wasted.

3. That the said child is without the proper parental care and guardianship in that the persons who have her care and custody are not the proper persons to been trusted with the rearing of such a child.

4. That the home in which the child is now being kept is an unfit place for such a child by reason of the neglect and depravity on the part of the person by whom she is kept.

5. That the guardian of the person and estate of said child is Peter Snyder and that she is now in the care and custody of Mr. and Mrs. Peter Snyder and resides at Red Fork, Oklahoma in Tulsa County.

6. That the said Mr. and Mrs. Peter Snyder are neither of them related to Sarah Ann Perryman in any degree; that they are living off of her estate and their only interest in said child is that they may have possession and control of her property.

7. That the next of kin of said child are Mrs. Buna Beaver, Mary Hearn, Bellie Hearn, and Demp Hearn, all of whom live at Tulsa, Oklahoma and to all of whom the said child bears the relation of half-sister.

8. That affidavit of Mrs. Buna Beaver is hereto attached and marked Exhibit "A" and made a part of this petition.

WHEREFORE, premises considered, your petitioner asks that summons issue forthwith and that the said child and those who have her in custody be brought before the Juvenile Court so that all matters set forth in this petition may be investigated; and that said child be adjudged a dependent and neglected child; that she be declared a ward of the Juvenile Court and that she be placed in such care and custody as may be found best suited to be her proper interest.

KATE BARNARD
Commissioner of Charities
And Corrections
By, Ross F. Lockridge,
General Attorney.
Ralsa F. Morley,
Assistant Counsel

WITNESSES:

Mrs. Buna Beaver, Tulsa, Oklahoma.

W. A. Sharp, Tulsa, Oklahoma.

R. P. Elliott, Tulsa, Oklahoma.

AFFIDAVIT.

Mrs. Buna Beaver, of lawful age, being duly sworn upon oath, says:

That she is acquainted with the child Sarah Ann Perryman; that she is a half-sister of said child and next of kin of said child; that the said child is an orphan child, both parents being dead; that the said child is eight years of age; that the said child since her infancy has been in the care and custody of Mr. and Mrs. Peter Snyder, and is at this time in the care and custody of Mr. and Mrs. Snyder; that Peter Snyder is at this time the guardian of the person and estate of said child and that the estate of said child, consisting of land and other interest in Tulsa County, has been and is being wasted and mismanaged under the charge of said Peter Snyder; that the said child is without the proper parental care and guardianship in that the said Peter Snyder and Mrs. Peter Snyder are improper parties for her care and custody and that their home is an unfit place tor the rearing of such a child; that they habitually use improper and profane language in the presence and hearing of said child and have become addicted to the use of profane language; that the said Mr. and Mrs. Peter Snyder frequently quarrel and fight in the home and have at various times separated from each other and have not given the said child the proper care and attention; that by reason of the habits and character of the said Mr. and Mrs. Snyder the home in which the child not being kept is an unfit place for the child and that in their care and keeping the said child is not developing good habits and good character and cannot, under such conditions, develop the right habits and character;

That the said Mr. and Mrs. Peter Snyder are living with the said child at Red Fork, Oklahoma, in Tulsa County; that their post office address is West Tulsa, Oklahoma; that the next of kin of said child are this affiant, Mrs. Buna Beaver, Mary Hearn, Bellis Hearn, and Demp Hearn, all of whom live at Tulsa, Oklahoma, and to all of who the said child bears the relation of half-sister; that neither Mr. or Mrs. Snyder are related to Sarah Ann Perryman either by consanguinity or affinity;

Affiant says that she makes this sworn complaint in the interest of said child and for the purpose of requesting and petitioning Kate Barnard, Commissioner of Charities and Corrections, to intervene as NEXT FRIEND on behalf of said child and to take such action as may be found necessary to place the child in proper custody and to protect her estate by a suitable guardianship;

Affiant says that all of the allegations herein are correct and true upon her best information and belief.

Mrs. Buna Beaver
Subscribed and sworn to before me this 8th day of March, 1913.
(Seal)Percy Collins,
Notary Public.
My Commission expires 11–27-1915

CHAPTER 18

Johnston County would have originally been under the protection of the Chickasaw Nation's Tishomingo County. It would have become Johnston, McLish, and Mosely counties in the Indian state of Sequoyah.

McClain County would have originally been under the protection of the Chickasaw Nation's Pontotoc County. It would have become Bonaparte and Garvin counties in the Indian state of Sequoyah.

McCurtain County would have originally been under the protection of the Choctaw Nation's Apukshunnubbee District in Nashoba, Boktoklo, Eagle, and Red River Counties. It would have become McCurtain County in the Indian state of Sequoyah.

Laston Coxwell, a Choctaw orphan, was owed $2,009.08. In 1915, a loaf of bread cost 7¢. If Laston ate a loaf a day it would have cost him approximately $25 a year.

JOHNSTON COUNTY

Lucinda Amos

Rosella Amos

Sallie Courtney

Willie Courtney

KAY COUNTY

James Poor-Horse

George Calls-Him

George Washington

Everett James

Alice Brewster

McCLAIN COUNTY

Oaklev

McCURTAIN COUNTY

Laston Coxwell: $2,009.08

Earnest Willie

CHAPTER 19

"Father, I need help. I am afraid that I will fight this thing and lose again. Everything is meaningless. Why do you not answer my people's cries for justice? I know that we as the Chahta have let corruption into our hearts and tribe. Is this why we are far from your heart? What of these white men? Are they not as corrupt and wicked as we are? Why do you favor them? You send the sun and rain on all but you let greed wash us away like a flood of hate. Our money builds their churches while ours dry on the vine. Is the Holy Spirit not the same for us? They have lied and stolen everything. They told us "forever," and now "forever" means that we will be strangers in our land. We are captives of our own poverty. I know that where fear is you are not, but why do you have us struggle against an enemy that you will not deliver us from? These men have money and power and will squash me. I feel in my heart that you want me to help Annie, yet you have given me nothing to fight for her. These men will not stop until they have stolen everything and they will crush her, and me also if we stand in their way. Is this what you want of me? I'm sorry to doubt you, Lord, and I'm sorry I am mad at you. You have told me to love my enemy and I am failing. Does loving them mean allowing them to rob and destroy the future of this little girl? Please father, please help me believe that you will be with me and not allow me to be overcome without an escape that you promise. Please, Father, help me help this little girl!"

Eben has been praying so hard that he is oblivious to everything until he hears the church bell. His eyes raise to see the little building and mothers moving their children from the porches of the camphouses towards the brush arbors with the benches under the shade. Coming towards him is little Annie.

"C'mon, Mr. Ben, c'mon. The church is starting," she says with cheeks round, brown, and beautiful.

"You go on, Whistle Britches, and I'll be right there."

Eben finally strolls to the arbor and manages to find a bench near a post. He leans against it as the service starts. Exia smiles at him as she sits down across the church altar platform on the female side. She looks particularly lovely this morning and Eben knows he is blessed. He then thinks about loss, about her being killed in this fight; he has to close his eyes and wish the paranoia away. The paranoia that something evil will take away the good; that the adversary will be allowed to toy with your life like Job.

Pastor Folsum prepares the group to sing and then opens with prayer. Soon the entire arbor is filled with prayer as everyone joins in concert, not loud, but a soft blanket of voice.

Pastor Folsum is already in his early sixties and his hearing is fading quickly. He preaches in a booming volume to hear himself. Apparently his employment at the saw mill has eroded more of his hearing than he is aware of. He is five-foot-three inches, and his slacks are too long, but not large enough in the waist. He has dapper, polished shoes, but his shirt is so tight in the neck that it is left open.

After singing the Choctaw version of "Press Along," and "Sinners Can You Hate Him?," the congregation grows silent.

"I will be reading from the story of Moses," he exhorts loudly and then pauses. "You know how you can tell God is about to move against a rebellious people, don't you? Every time the Bible talks about children dying at the hands of someone wicked, you know God will move. Pharaoh kills the firstborn, and God delivers Moses! Herod kills the firstborn, and God delivers Jesus! Brothers and sisters, God is the same today as he was yesterday. Amen?!

As Pastor Folsum continues to read from the Scripture, he builds momentum and paints a complete mental image of how Christ blesses the little children by patting some of the children on the head. His oration speaks about caring for the innocent, of holiness and holy duty. He wipes his brow in contemplation, hushing to hear the whisper of the spirit.

"My friend, Cubbin Ludlow, preaches over near Honobia. He told me about having to do a funeral for a little girl who lived over near Smithville. No one had seen her for a few months after her dad had died. Her mother had disappeared and folks said that maybe she just abandoned this little girl. Her grandma took her in and was trying to take care of her. Daddy and momma gone. Fearing a court-appointed guardian, Grandma took that baby to Wheelock. The guardian came in and took that baby out of school, out of protection. They found that little girl starved to death in that house across the river, back where the old stand of pine is near that town."

The Pastor strolls back and forth behind the makeshift pulpit, storing energy and immersing his mind in solitude. Then he continues. "That little girl, as it turns out, had an allotment worth money. You know how the white man carved up our land, putting some families' lands here and others there, at first we all talked like the white man was crazy because he couldn't keep families straight so that all their lands could be right next to each other. You know, so the entire family could help watch over it. Well, I tell you, they weren't crazy. They were like the wolves Jesus spoke about, how they get in the flock and separate. You see, if that girl's land was next to her family's, then everyone in the family would have been able to see what was going on. You know what was going on? She was making money and didn't even know it!

"That little girl was worth nearly two hundred thousand dollars when she died. You know who got the money? Some man up near Poteau. She starved to death while some person called a guardian held her money. She died lonely because her parents were gone. I bet her momma just didn't disappear. Who knows? Jesus knows! Amen?

"The Lord sees everything and we know that all things will be called into account. Brothers and sisters, whatever you do to the least of these you have done to me! Amen? I heard about people being blown up for oil money up north. The times are wicked! How many of you remember back when some of those men would come and run through our church meetings with their horses? That's why this church moved from in town at Nashoba over to here, remember? Remember how they would ride in the middle of the night and turn over beds out on the porches during the summer and scare us half to death? They knew Choctaw sleep outside in the summer! Do you think they got lost at midnight? No they were trying to make us want to move, to abandon our hard work for them to inherit, land already cleared for farming.

"Now children are dying for money! You can't serve God and money, amen?! Sometimes I wish we would have done what Jacob Jackson wanted us to do and move our people to Mexico, maybe there we could have lived in peace! But we didn't and now it is up to us, the remnant, to provide for the protection of the innocent. We are going to raise money here at this church to protect those who need it. That little girl there will not die of starvation or neglect. The collection we take up will help protect her. How you ask? We will use it to send Brother Baker to help her.

"The churches that Paul started would send money for the poor in Jerusalem and we will send money for the poor to not be trampled on. Brothers and sisters do not give grudgingly."

Eben gawks dumbstruck at Pastor Folsum. He knows God has given his answer—make your way to Nineveh, or risk being carried by a mountain lion.

CHAPTER 20

Tams Bixby had been the Republican delegate for the Oklahoma Enabling Act. Henry Rogers, the attorney and former land man for McMan Oil, would successfully be elected to the Oklahoma House of Representatives for the Tulsa district as a Republican. Henry Rogers was the Vice President of Union National Bank in Tulsa. The Attorney, L. B. Jackson of Sapulpa, who was cited in the case, was also a Vice President of Union National Bank.

McMan Oil was founded by James Chapman and Robert McFarlin in Holdenville, Oklahoma. The joint venture was originally Holdenville Oil & Gas Company. McFarlin was a noted philanthropist, helping build the opera house in Holdenville as well as starting three churches and four schools. McFarlin was so wary of Holdenville and the boom camps at the time, he made sure his wife lived safely in Norman, the home of the University of Oklahoma. Indeed McFarlin bankrolled the building of the Norman Methodist Episcopal Church. He and his wife gave extensively to the Southern Methodist University in Texas, building the McFarlin Auditorium. The McFarlins also built the library for Tulsa University.

Tulsa University was founded by the Muscogee Nation as Henry Kendall College for the education of Muscogee daughters to become teachers. Tulsa University, as a Presbyterian-based college, does not acknowledge that the Muscogee Nation founded it.

Malone v. Scott was decided on June 20, 1916, in the Supreme Court of Oklahoma. It read:

> ¶1 This is an action brought by the plaintiffs in error against the defendants in error, to recover the lands, and to remove clouds upon the title thereof, described in the petition. The lands in question were the allotment of Ullie Eagle, deceased, a full-blood Creek citizen. There were several interveners, and cross-petitions were filed which we deem unnecessary to recite, other than

the cross-petition filed by L. W. Jones, as guardian *ad litem* of the defendant. Hepsie Mitchell, an incompetent, in which said cross-petition it was alleged that Hepsie Mitchell was the sole and surviving heir at law of the said Ullie Eagle, and that, as such heir of Ullie Eagle, she took, by the law of descent and distribution then in force, the fee-simple title to all the real estate described in the said petition. The case was tried to the court, and the court found Nellie Fish, one of the defendants, to be the sole heir at law of Ullie Eagle, deceased, of the land in controversy, and that the defendants, James H. Chapman and Montfort Jones, are the grantees of Nellie Fish and have a right of possession of the premises described in their cross-petition, subject to a certain oil and gas mining lease upon said lands, which it is unnecessary to describe, and that the said defendants, including the said Hepsie Mitchell, have no right, title, or interest in the land, and rendered judgment accordingly, on the 8th day of October, 1914. To reverse the judgment rendered, the plaintiffs in error prosecute, by transcript, this appeal.

¶2 On April 7, 1915, which was within one day of the six months in which appeal could be taken, summons in error issued to Hepsie Mitchell, an incompetent, and to Levi W. Jones as her guardian *ad litem*, directed to the sheriff of Creek county, Okla., and on the 12th day of April, 1915, return was made by said sheriff of said summons in error that "Hepsie Mitchell and Levi W. Jones, as her guardian *ad litem*, not found in Creek county." On the 5th day of June, 1915, an affidavit was filed by Roman Tiger to obtain service by publication of said summons in error upon said Hepsie Mitchell and Levi W. Jones, her guardian *ad litem*, "averring that service of summons cannot be made upon said defendants with due diligence; that said defendants have departed from said county to avoid the service of said summons." Publication of said summons in error was made and proof of said publication of said summons in error was filed with the clerk of this court on March 27, 1916, showing that said summons was first published in the Creek County Republican on June 18, 1915. On May 10, 1916, James A. Chapman and Montfort Jones, appearing especially for the purpose of moving the court to dismiss the appeal, filed a motion to dismiss this appeal upon the ground that Hepsie Mitchell and Levi W. Jones, as guardian *ad litem*, were necessary parties to the proceedings in error in this cause, and had not been served with summons in error. It is unquestioned that summons in error in this cause was never personally served upon Hepsie Mitchell, or her guardian, Levi W. Jones, and that the attempted service by publication was not first published until after more than 60 days after the time in which the appeal in this case could be taken had expired.

¶3 The first question to be determined is whether or not the said Hepsie Mitchell and her guardian, Levi W. Jones, are necessary parties to this appeal. Second, was the summons in error to Hepsie Mitchell and Levi W. Jones legally served by publication? These questions will be considered in their order.

¶6 In Bilby v. Woodward et al., 47 Okla. 122, 148 P. 96, the syllabus is as follows: "Where an Indian minor, by his guardian, sued several defendants to quiet title to his allotment, and a third party intervened and claimed to be the sole owner thereof and prayed for like relief, and where said minor prevailed and his title thereto was quieted, and one of the defendants and the intervener bring the case here without joining the other defendants, held, that those defendants are necessary parties, and must either make a general appearance in this court within the time allowed by law for appealing from said decree, or summons must issue within such time and service thereon be had, or the appeal will be dismissed."

¶11 The said Hepsie Mitchell being a necessary party to this appeal, and not having been served, either personally or by publication, with a summons in error, this court is without jurisdiction. "All persons who are parties to the proceeding in the trial court, and whose interests will be affected by a reversal of the judgment on appeal, must be properly brought in and made parties in the appellate court, or the proceeding will be dismissed." Boyd v. Robinson, 47 Okla. 591, 149 P. 1146; Thompson et al. v. Fulton, 29 Okla. 700, 119 P. 244; K. C. & M. & O. Ry. Co. v. Williams, 33 Okla. 202, 124 P. 63; American National Bank v. Linotype Co., 31 Okla. 533 122 P. 507; Bowles v. Cooney et al., 45 Okla. 517, 146 P. 221.

¶12 This appeal should be dismissed.

¶13 By the Court: It is so ordered.

CHAPTER 21

Almost all tribes in the southeast thought of the sun as a deity. Not a male one, but a female. Many of the Muscogee called her Sister Sun and the Moon was Brother. The Euchee call the Sun Grandmother. At one time the Choctaw word for God was *Hashtali*. *Hashhee* means "the Sun." You could think of tribal towns as denominations of sorts. Each one had its own unique version of common worship. In the twentieth century, Muscogee women began using turtle shells fastened to the tops of old cowboy boots, thus recycling their husband's old worn-out boots. Sometime in the mid-twentieth century some began attaching small milk cans with pebbles inside to replace the turtles. Of course many centuries before the women attached layered deer hoofs to make the cadence of the dance.

Almost all Christian denominations celebrate a form of communion, but it doesn't all look the same. At the beginning of the new year in July, all Muscogee families would light their fires from one fire; incendiary communion. European missionaries were able to connect the southeastern tribal understanding of fire to Christianity. The missionaries understood that the fire symbolized in part the life-giving nature of the sun. Worship involving fire has a fancy European word called "pyrolatry." The missionaries found a bridge. They said to the Muscogee that God had spoken through a fire to one of their greatest leaders; ironically, they didn't mention he was not European. The missionaries illustrated that through that fire Moses established their religion. God speaking in the flames. Illumination was not a new concept to the spiritual Muscogee.

McIntosh County would have originally been under the protection of the Muscogee Nation's Eufaula District. It would have become Eufaula, a portion of Muscogee and Cussehta counties in the Indian state of Sequoyah.

Marshall County would have originally been under the protection of the Chickasaw Nation's Pickens County. It would have become San Bois and Thomas counties in the Indian state of Sequoyah.

Mayes County would have originally been under the protection of the Cherokee Nation's Cooweescoowee District. It would have become Tumechichee and Mayes counties in the Indian state of Sequoyah.

McINTOSH COUNTY

Lofa Manlcv: $500.00

Earle Mitchel

Posey Mitchel

Phoebe Mitchel

Opal Mitchel

Clementina Green

Albert Grayson

Willie Jackson

Laston Coxwell

Louie Coxwell

MARSHALL COUNTY

Benjamin Robinson

Ester Robinson

Tilman Robinson

Caroline Robinson: $553.43

Amos Robinson

Mary Ann Robinson

Moss Ned

Joseph Anoatubby

Apala Anoatubby

Lena Anoatubby

Joseph Anoatubby

Apola Anoatubby

Lena Anoatubby

Emma Lawrence: $276.75

Ida Anoatubby $630.00

Abner Anoatubby $630.00

MAYES COUNTY

Christiana B. Crittendent

Cullen T Bryant, et al

Bertha L. Brown

Fannie M. Brown

Saddie M. Brown

CHAPTER 22

Sequoyah had invented an alphabet after viewing the talking leaves of the white man. History records that he marveled at the written communication and realized it was a key to his people's survival. Salvation by adaptation is the mantra that became the genesis of the Cherokee syllabary. The five tribes attempted a political maneuver in his name to survive by adaptation. Everyone at the Sequoyah convention spoke of the impending state of Oklahoma like the apocalypse.

Eben also became emotional about the impending avaricious cataclysm and he could see opportunists licking their mineral-craved lips. He watched tribal politicians implement a brilliant but ill-timed plan. They drafted a single Constitution with representatives chosen by established tribal counties, which would make the five tribes a union and ensure county and ultimately tribal polity changed, but guaranteeing representation. Eben is pragmatic and knew that the American nation would not let them easily morph into the federal union. Echoes of Mississippi and removal sounded like the nuance of the new state name "Oklahoma" which ironically means "red people," a state whose sole purpose is to destroy them. Eben is suspicious that the power brokers in the five tribes are more interested in saving their own power than rescuing the people. If the gamble had paid off there would never have been an Okie from Muskogee.

Eben, barely the Okie, steps from the wagon, tired from the trip and the growing knot where his stomach is. When you are on new terrain that seems familiar it is difficult to feign composure. If this town had been the capitol city of Sequoyah he may have stood a chance; after all he knew how to maneuver politically in the Choctaw Nation. The knot of trepidation is more about not knowing what invisible forces control the rules. There is the law and then that invisible code where male fraternities exchange justice based on patronage and heredity; very much like the Choctaw, just with pinker skins.

The brand new Muskogee courthouse gleams in the sun. In his mind the contrast is stark; he had traveled from a community of believers who had built a one-room, wooden-shingled building, not much more than a square box. Here is the woodland bumpkin standing before a marbled edifice a hundred times larger. He couldn't help but think "David wasn't scared, my butt!" He begins a ritual of self-motivation, a kind of pep talk between himself and God: "I'm going in and I will walk up the stairs to the second floor. I will ask to speak with the royalty division. I will ask to see the file for the Individual Indian Money Account for Annie. Simple, and I will be through in an hour." He smiles at the absurdity of the plan. He has no money to bribe or berate. Poor folk have poor ways.

His legs, weighted with anxiety, begin stepping up the north marble stair case to the second floor, the smell of sweat already salting his nostrils. "I probably will look and smell like a wet dog by the time I get there," he thinks.

A rather gaunt Ichabod-looking official sits in his chair, reviewing correspondence, then lifts his head sharply, looking out the half-door at Eben. Eben begins faking a half-smile, the kind that says, "Don't be alarmed. I am not a wagon-burner."

Suddenly the man utters, "Can I help you?," but with a voice that sounds like a principal ready to administer swats.

Eben replies cheerily, "I would like the directions to a Royalty Officer."

"Whom would you like to speak to?"

"Anyone would be fine," Eben counters like a drone bee trying to read the dance of a guard.

"I'm afraid that without a name it will be pointless, since we do not provide meetings without advance notice." The first bureaucratic obstacle and the principal knows it is a doozy. This is the era before regular Indians are considered customers.

Eben smiles, nods, and begins walking down the stairs. He is already thinking of his excuses to Pastor Folsum and Dicey, and then he thinks of his wife. She will read him like a book. He will not be able to avoid the messy questions. An epiphany comes to him on the eighth step as he descends: "Sneak past the principal, find a closet to hide in, and then pilfer through the files after hours." Then logic counters with the image of federal marshals grabbing him, beating him, and then stuffing him into a cell that is danker than the closet. The anxiety of the eighth step is so heavy the granite weighs on his chest. Suddenly his resolve turns on and tunes out the storm of doubt and he turns and heads back up the stairs.

The principal looks even more discouraging on the second approach. Eben then finds that segment of a man's heart that wants confrontation, tightens his face, and begins his approach.

"My name is Eben Baker and I represent the aunt of Annie Meshaya, an Indian ward. I assume her property is worth a substantial amount of funds otherwise there would not be lawyers involved. It is my assumption that you will be able to direct me to who can tell me the companies leasing her property. I know that your Royalty Division will have the names of the principals who have controlling interest in the mineral company that possess the lease. I'm betting that the company has some relationship to one of the rail companies that I collected against when I was in the Choctaw Nation treasury."

The principal's face changes into an expression of masked approval. "Well I assume you have the legal description of the property?"

"I would have it if that attorney from Wilburton hadn't blocked me from obtaining it." Eben instantly wishes he hadn't played that card of declaring his preceding obstacles. The next minute seems to congeal and the aroma of buttermilk pervades the intervening stare contest. And then the principal blinked!

"What did you say the girl's name was?" The principal shifts from his seat to begin walking his orientation towards a row of six wooden file cabinets.

"Annie Meshaya."

"What is her age?"

"She is ten years old."

"I of course will have a record of her property, but that will only be informative as to the property description. Leasehold interests will be maintained by the Royalty Division. I assume that the last name Meshaya means that this girl is Choctaw?" The principal is peering over his metal rims with his chin doubling.

"She is Choctaw." Eben is assessing the next volley, his tongue reined.

The principal resumes filtering through the third file cabinet third row down. As he scans he is butchering the pronunciations, names dormant now like "Felikatubee" or "Nashobabilili," names hard earned on the field of battle now imprisoned in cellulose jackets typed in courier font.

"According to this Dawes census card Annie is the daughter of Sukey and Elijah Meshaya, and this card shows that she is enrolled as a minor at the age of one. The card number is forty three fifty two conducted at Red Oak." The principal walks across the room and sets the card on the half-door shelf.

Eben looks down at the card and there "Elijah Meshaya of Red Oak and his wife Sukey" is listed on the line below where the lines and margins form a column of boxes for individual names, and her hometown of Nashoba leaps out at Eben. Annie is listed as born in Red Oak. In the jacket are several other documents that are accidentally or purposefully misfiled. One document lists a Dawes Clerk named Robert Morgan. Eben procures a piece of paper from his pocket and begins jotting down the card number and the Dawes Clerk's name. Déjà vu overtakes him. The principal stares intently at Eben when he lifts his face from the documents.

"Kinda jumps out at ya doesn't it?" The principal is stone-faced serious.

"*Yakoke*. 'Thank you' in my language."

"If this ends up like I think it will, you will no longer thank me." The principal closes the jacket and carries it back to join the countless others.

"I'm sorry, but I didn't ask your name."

"I would prefer that my name did not come up."

"No, I don't want it to get you in trouble. I just want your first name, and I want to give it to my church to pray for you."

The principal looks at Eben with astonishment. "My name is Tom."

"Thank you, Tom."

As Eben leaves the office he thinks about Tom and prays. Angels sometimes look like principals. What he doesn't know is that the BIA has already approved 4,366 oil and gas leases and Annie's is but one.

CHAPTER 23

On February 14th, 1914, Congress began investigation of Indian Children probate cases. Largely because of the efforts of Kate Barnard. She lobbied everyone she could and spoke at the Mohonk conference seeking alliances. The Congressional Record retained the debates from her investigations:

> Mr. CAMPBELL of Kansas: Mr. Chairman, the consideration of the Indian appropriation bill naturally brings us to a discussion of the Indian question. I have stated upon this floor upon other occasions that ·I protested against the attitude of the white man toward the Indian from the beginning of our relations with the Indian in the United States. From the first there has been a disregard of the rights of the inferior that has been unbecoming of the people of this Republic, and the attitude of mind toward the rights of the Indian has not grown better as time has gone on.
>
> We have moved the Indian from one lodging place to another, and have practically forced him into treaties that would enable us to move him. We sought the treaty and forced the Indian to enter into it just as soon as his lands became desirable for the use of the white man. And we finally moved him to the last place in which there was a Territory within the confines of that vast domain that had belonged to the Indian, and located him in a small strip known as the Indian Territory, where we entered into a solemn treaty with the Indians that they should not be disturbed there by the white man. That treaty had no limitations as to time. As long as grass grew and water ran, the Indian was to have absolute dominion over the Indian Territory and the protection of the white man.
>
> Those of you who were here yesterday listened to a speech that disclosed the fact that the Indian Territory no longer belongs to the Indian, but to the white man; and legislation was asked in the

interests of the white man in the use of the "Indian's" money or what he has left. In consideration of Indian matters, within my experience in this House the interest of the white man has been made paramount to the interest of the Indian. That attitude upon the part of Congress was not directed or led by men far removed from the last place that had been allotted to the American Indian in the United States. White men from the Indian Territory acted without regard to the rights of the Indian, always having foremost in their minds, the rights of the white man who had protruded himself into the Indian Territory. And today it is a joke to refer to the Indian Territory as Indian country, if a joke can be made of such a serious matter, and a matter that so reflects upon the honor of this Government in its treatment of a homeless, courageous race of men that we have driven from one place to another until they have practically vanished.

The treaty of 1836 gave the Territory of Oklahoma as a final place of habitation for the American Indian, and it did not include the State of Kansas. It included what is known as the Indian Territory, and it was made sacred in that treaty to the Indians.

Mr. MURRAY of Oklahoma: (Mr. Murray was Alfalfa Bill Murray, who had been the Attorney for the Chickasaw Nation and also on the state of Sequoyah effort) Mr. Chairman, will the gentleman yield just a moment for a correction?

The CHAIRMAN: Does the gentleman yield?

Mr. CAMPBELL: I do.

Mr. MURRAY: There were several of those treaties that the gentleman refers to?

Mr. CAMPBELL: Yes.

Mr. MURRAY: They ran for a period of years?

Mr. CAMPBELL: Yes.

Mr. MURRAY: And included the whole of Oklahoma, except the Panhandle strip?

Mr. CAMPBELL: Yes; that is true. Now the Indian is a helpless ward. We are giving him out his own in driblets, not as his necessities require, but as our interests and the interests of the white man seem to dictate. Will it be beneficial to the white farmers of Oklahoma to put the Indian's money within reach *of* the Indian?

Will it be beneficial to the white people of Oklahoma to do something for the Indian? If not, God help the Indian! Nothing will be done for him. The first consideration is the benefit that may result to the white man who has taken from the Indian his dominions in the United States. I am not charging anybody in particular with this. I simply charge it upon our Government, and its treatment of these now helpless men. The present appropriation bill has recognized the fact that we have not only been treating the Indian in this manner, but that we have been plundering him of his property.

Mr. GREEN of Iowa: Was any appropriation made in this bill for an examination of those claims?

Mr. CAMPBELL: No. We did not appropriate in this bill other claims. That is a matter that is to be taken into consideration in a separate bill that will probably be called the omnibus claims bill.

The white man in Oklahoma has reserved or assumed the right to take everything belonging to the Indian that he could get his hands on. He entered into contracts with the Indian that were indefensible, and which the courts would not have sustained because of fraud if the contracts had been entered into by one white man with another. Every species of fraud and intimidation has been practiced by white men on Indians in Oklahoma. Courts and court officers have been used to rob helpless children of the last bit of property that they possessed. Children who had estates that were considered valuable, whose assent could not be secured to sell or lease their property, were murdered, and contracts made with the executors of their estates, and the murderers went unpunished by the authorities in the communities in which the murders were committed. I have protested against this attitude for years, and—

Mr. DAVENPORT: Mr. Chairman, will the gentleman yield for a question?

The CHAIRMAN: Does the gentleman yield?

Mr. CAMPBELL: Just for a question.

Mr. DAVENPORT: I would like to ask the gentleman what murder was committed?

Mr. CAMPBELL: I think it was in the congressional district which the gentleman represents.

Mr. DAVENPORT: Please wait for my question. What murder was committed for an estate of any child in any county in Oklahoma and the murderer went unpunished, giving the name of the child and the name of the party that committed the murder?

Mr. CAMPBELL: The murder was in the district represented by the gentleman, and the murderer went unwhipped for his offense until an appropriation was made in this House to send special agents to the place of the murder, who forced the local authorities to indict and convict the party.

Mr. DAVENPORT: I will say to the gentleman that if he does not know that that statement is correct he ought not to make it on this floor, and I say to him now it is untrue. I say, that the officers in Muskogee County, if he has reference to that case that occurred at Taft-that nigger town down there in Muskogee County-did perform every duty in their power to capture that man.

Mr. ADAIR: I want to ask for information if the remedy for this mistreatment of the Indians rests with the Interior Department or does it rest with Congress itself?

Mr. CAMPBELL: With both, and with the American people, with the white man. That is where it rests, with those who have totally disregarded all the rights of a now helpless people, with a disregard that has become more and more a shame to the white man as the years have come and gone. Ever since Oklahoma was admitted as a State this question has become more and more acute. I have read from time to time that local courts, fresh from the electorate in Oklahoma, were aiding and abetting those who were plundering helpless Indians—incompetent Indians and Indian children—of their property. It was denied. Charges were made that I was making these charges against the officers in Oklahoma for political effect. I was making these charges against the officers in Oklahoma in the hope that someday the people of this country and the people of Oklahoma would be aroused to the fact that it was wrong to rob the Indians. For years it has not been regarded as a crime to rob and take advantage of the Indian, especially in Oklahoma. I am gratified now to be able to tell the House that the things for which a few of us have been contending here are now conceded by the Members of the Oklahoma delegation to be right, and they are assenting to the appropriation which is included in this bill that is necessary for the protection of helpless wards of this Government known as incompetent Indians and minor Indian children.

Mr. CARTER: Mr. Chairman, the gentleman from Kansas [Mr. CAMPBELL] seems to take great delight in trying to discredit his next-door neighbors, the good people of Oklahoma and their Congressmen, and would seem to like to have this House believe that all the thieves, robbers, grafters, and debauchers of Indians have congregated for their last harbor of refuge in the State of Oklahoma.

Let the gentleman look a little to his own State. Let him remember that at one time practically the entire State of Kansas was owned by the Indians. Unfortunately, the aborigine has been dispossessed in that State until he now owns less than four-tenths of 1 per cent of the land in that entire great State, and what has Poor Lo to show for it? That there has been some fraud with relation to probate matters in Oklahoma no one attempts to deny, and I have never attempted to deny it in the past, but I defy the gentleman to mention a case in which the culprit has gone unpursued or to give any evidence on behalf of his statement that his punishment was not due to the diligence of the authorities of the State of Oklahoma. We have 40 counties on the eastern side of the State of Oklahoma with more than 101,000 allottees, and it is but natural that some percentage of fraud and some irregularities should be possible under such complicated conditions as these. The attention of this House has only been called to two cases of fraud in deceased estates in the district which I have the honor to represent.

One of these was the case of Judge Phillips at Durant, Oklahoma, and these charges were made upon testimony of a very personal friend of the distinguished gentleman from Kansas. His name is Jim Yarborough, and, by the way, Jim is a bully fellow. He is an A-1 boy to have with you in a campaign, as the gentleman from Kansas has found out, for he often has Jim Yarborough up in his district campaigning for him when he has a close race.

Mr. CAMPBELL: Very well. I will ask the Chair to call my attention when I have consumed seven or eight minutes. The gentleman from Oklahoma [Mr. CARTER] referred to the testimony of Mr. Yarborough as though that testimony was largely the result of the witness's imagination. Here is what he testified to:

Chickie-Chockie, an Indian, owned a tract of land within the jurisdiction of the Bryan County court that was renting for $300 a year. There was a total of 325 acres. The land sold for $400, and the court approved the sale.

The gentleman from Oklahoma [Mr. CARTER] heard that testimony some three years ago. He also heard the testimony given as to the Bryan County court, and I will put the whole of this in the —, but to save time I will read:

Ike Poole was the guardian of Summie Poole. Now, Summie had considerable property. She was an Indian child, eight years old. The guardian sold her property. The aggregate of the sale was $2,830.75. Ike Poole, the guardian of this little child, appointed by the court, brought in a bill of expenses for $4,067.70. The court, after seriously considering the matter, reduced the amount of that claim $75, leaving a balance due the guardian of $2,136.55. The child owed its guardian $2,136.55. A petition was filed to have the homestead of the child sold to pay the amount of this $2,136.55. The court approved the report of the guardian.

Mr. CARTER: Will the gentleman yield?

Mr. CAMPBELL: Yes.

Mr. CARTER: I believe I stated those were the two cases I knew of.

Mr. CAMPBELL: Yes.

(After ongoing debate)

Mr. MANN: —I think it is proper to say that although the entire delegation last April urged the governor to have this telegram read before both houses of the Oklahoma Legislature, which I assume was done, asking for remedial legislation, and making the statement which I think the gentleman from Oklahoma [Mr. CARTER] read, that the Oklahoma delegation could not expect to get title legislation desired here unless the Oklahoma Legislature would grant remedial legislation as to probate courts. Some gentlemen now say that the Mott report–and the gentleman from Oklahoma this morning said that Mr. Mott's statements would not be believed in Oklahoma. Mr. Mott's statements, in my judgment are believed in Oklahoma by the honest people there.

[Mr. Mott is the National Attorney for the Muscogee Nation]

The report dated December 31, 1913, contains this language:

The commissioner then touched on a convention to be held in Muskogee, Oklahoma, to which he goes from here, and which is to take up the matter of guardianship of Indian minors on the reservations and the administration of their estates.

Then the commissioner said:

The Indian children of Oklahoma are the richest average children in the United States. However, it is a lamentable fact that they have less statutory protection there than in any other State. In the 40 counties in eastern Oklahoma there are now pending from 800 to 1,500 probate estates, about 85 per cent of which are Indian children's estates.

I have recently discovered that it costs about 3 percent to settle a white child's estate and that it costs more than 20 percent to settle the estate of an Indian boy or girl. This is the result of guardians having been appointed without regard to their equipment and the acceptance of bondsmen many times wholly insolvent. Enormous fees have been charged by attorneys and unconscionable fees by guardians, together with indefensible expenditures of their funds, which has frequently resulted in the dissipation of their entire property.

It is not an uncommon thing when an Indian child reaches his majority to find that his guardian has absconded and that his bondsmen are wholly financially irresponsible. It is my determined intention to reform this indefensible condition, and to this end I have recently appointed a number of probate attorneys who will give their whole time, under my direction, to this work.

CHAPTER 24

Sealie was listed as 90 years old on the Dawes Census Card which was done March 13, 1902, the same year Ullie was hanged. Ullie was age eight at the time. This means several things. Sealie was either Ullie's great-grandmother or great-great-grandmother. Sealie was born in Alabama and was from Artussee Tribal Town. Sealie was an infant when the Muscogee people were invaded by Tennessee volunteers under the command of General Jackson. Sealie survived the War of 1812. Sealie survived the Creek Civil War that followed. Sealie survived the Trail of Tears, where infants and the elderly fell like leaves in the cold wind. Sealie survived the grueling march when over 4,000 of her fellow Muscogee people had died. Sealie survived the US Civil War when 3,500 Muscogee warriors joined the Union and 1,375 joined the Confederacy. Tustanuc Hajo is listed in the 1st Indian Home Guard, and the same name is listed as her father on the census card. Maybe it was her brother or a relative? Sealie had survived so much tragedy. It is beyond ironic that Sealie's and Ullie's tribal enrollment for their allotment was completed during the Ides of March.

Muskogee County would have originally been under the protection of the Muscogee Nation's Muskogee District. It would have become Muscogee and a portion of Eufaula County in the Indian state of Sequoyah. In Muscogee County, American Indian minors would be owed over $13,364,760.40 to buy food.

MUSKOGEE COUNTY

Joe Bruner

Ruby Coffee

Violett Coffee

Lennie Rogers

James H. Lynch

John T. Lynch

Alberta Jones: $539.20

Washington Harrison: $202.37

Nettie Harrison: $152.01

Dewey Harrison: $200.14

Sanders Henderson: $609.09

Doctor Barnett: $480.00

Noovella Bell: $2172.00

Iosall Lyons: $196.70

Vandervelt Lewis: $896.00

Clarence Sango: $309.01

Clarence Sango: $1,400.00

Jerry Grayson

George Grayson

Mai B. Robbins: $284.05

Everette E. Robbins 248.04

Lena N. Robbins: $269.28

Richard R. Robbins: $193.25

Dewit Caesar: $240.00

Annie Scott: $80.00

Alex Scott: $160.00

Barney McKellop: $1,479.00

Sam Sango: $60.00

Viola Sango: $160.00

Anna A. Smith: $418.40

Reno Allen

Jack Madden: $1,865.04

Clarence Madden: $1,660.10

Howard Madden: $1,862.13

Robert T. Garner: $605.77

Please Lee: $948.65

Tom Monday: $80.00

Jesse Monday: $240.00

Clayton Monday: $240.00

Margerete Berry: $122.50

Dereaver Berry: $924.05

Walter Berry: $2,229.56

Rebecca Coody: $249.27

David Leader: $340.00

Levi Peters: $95.17

Joseph Leader: $340.00

Theodore Watson: $525.00

Tonny Latty: $182.02

Betsy Rich

Nee Latty: $387.02

Frank Young: $1,600.00

Lillian Lewis T.: $1,493.83

Oscar Mickens: $1,690.47

Walter Mickens: $180.50

Walter Mickens, et al: $6,500.00

Sarah Waters: $1,127.50

Annie Waters: $1,127.50

Maude Foreman: $249.44

George Foreman

C. Foreman: $349.37

William Cendy, Jr: $13.50

Sarah Peters: $128.72

Washington Lowe: $558.90

Sadie Charles: $2,876.40

Jackson Hood: $201.05

William Hood: $37.56

John Hood: $238.32

James Hood

Elnora Benge: $3,618.40

Orline Benge: $2,690.08

Pearl Hill: $1,401.25

George Hill: $1.981 .04

Richard Delwood: $330.25

Eva Dorcas Murphy: $490.67

Sidney Johnson: $1, 197.77

Ralph Mayson: $2,215.00

Mary Choteau, now Mary Hall: $431.88

Lidia Stewart: $193.75

Jane Hammer: $100.00

Eliza Hammer: $200.00

Mary E. Hammer: $200.00

Josie Hammer: $120.00

John Mcintosh: $3.523.00

Hewitt C. Howdeshell: 280.00

Minnie J. Howdeshell: $285.00

Leo Ampach: $301.50

Louis McNach: 135.95

Joe Bishop: $459.00

Samuel E. Roberts: $109.30

Nancy Peters

Alice Weber: $396.00

Everett W. Jones: $228.77

Peggy Sewell: $160.00

Manuel Monday: $100.00

Willie Mcintosh: $337.85

Sallie Hodge: $21,635.15

Minnie Beaver: $111.73

Emma London

Washington Drew: $2,930.42

Roxana Drew: $3,025.25

Norah Harmer: $652.64

Mamie Harmer: $918.54

LeRoy Harmer: $1,072.06

George Harmer: $1,072.06

Berry Monday: $165.00

Ellis Canard: $164.70

Henry Reynolds

Lilburn Reynolds

Hanson Newens: $750.00

John Davis Richardson

John Anderson: $208.50

Claude D. Marris: $2,787.71

Pearl L. Marris: $467.01

Jessie M. Marris: $2,409.65

Bertha L. Marris: $2,109.97

Arthur R. Marris: $412.28

Reno Wilson

Rena Williams: $118.20

Simon Garagan

Tom Davis: $431.20

Thersa Sherman: $840.00

Anna Sherman: $439.00

Lilly Sherman: $770.00

May Moore

Tina Moore: $165.00

Fanella Moore

Bertie Moore

Tommie Williams: $508.53

James Thompson

Viola Edwards: $3,066.63

LeRoy Edwards: $8,803.88

Johnnie Peters: $70.00

James Griffin: $15.00

John Griffin: $510.00

Addie Griffin

Lewis Griffin

William L. Foreman: $800.00

Olga C. Nelson: $12.00

Eva E. Nelson: $12.00

Irving (Yabola) Posey: $2,530.00

Wynema T. Posev: $1,765.00

La Vanch Battenfield: $1,000.00

Ben Jackson: $133.33

Grady Jackson: $133.33

Fannv Bell Jackson: $133.33

Ada Cordrev: $1,225.00

John Thomas Burke: $8,835.69

Cvnda Sango: $718.79

Catherine Perry: $143.21

Julius Perry: $182.43

Corah Hayes

Stella Hayes

Luther G. Rowe: $689.94

Charles Nave: $327.76

Thomas G. Nave

Margaret O. Nave: $229.91

William Nave: $373.17

Charles Nave

Wil!iam Nave

Margaret O. Nave

Emma Walker

Grace Smith: $820.00

Clara Tavlor: $3,248.50

Floyd E. Taylor: $3,248.50

Lawrence Taylor: $3,248.50

Rena Allen

Israel Lyons: $251.70

George Smith: $812.56

Pearlie Smith: $82126

Louis L. Miller

Chute Miller: $220.41

Jack Blythe: $126.95

Charles Miller: $137.13

Theodore R. Miller

Pearle Samuels

Pearl Samuels: $3,500.00

Freeland Johnson: $1,943.65

Washington Johnson: $1,763.82

Klie Bolin: $7,283.08

Florence Norris: $912.81

Jessie Johnson: $1,125.61

Laura Dean

Bennie Gilcrease: $3765.53

Florence Gilcrease: $1,705.62

Lena Gilcrease

Lennie Robinson

David Archibald

Abel Archibald

Cain Archibald

Etta Archibald

Maggie Wilson

Johnie Wilson

James Edmond Doherty

Lethia Doherty

Ella M. Doherty

William L. Doherty

Elizabeth Caroline Doherty

Frank M. Schonover

Ettie J. Webb: $660.78

Ethel S. Webb: $732.46

Fannie White: $141.10

Jonny Island: $1,292.94

Laura Johnson

Clara Johnson

Ivia Johnson

Flora Holcomb

Jacob Holcomb

Richard Holcomb

Charles Jacob

Emma Jacobs

Jessie M. Shipp

Willie B. Shipp

Harold Blessing

Gracie Hawkins: $3,200.00

Gracie Hawkins: $3,200.00

Major Wiley: $3,713.65

Alberta Durant: $253.98

Roxie Durant: $253.98

Romeo W. Jefferson: $800.00

Dora Ellen Parks: $1,474.76

Dora Ellen Parks2: $1,700.52

Wesley Washington: $1,245.38

Jacob Sells: $187.50

Willie Sells: $250.00

Gracie Sells: $250.0c

Floyd Freeman

John Anna Johnson

Gracie M. Johnson: $4.170.00

Lafayette L. Johnson

Lena Scott: $120.00

Mattie A. Mathews: $317.71

Rena Mathews: $600.18

John Andrew Mathews: $593.83

Tommie Newman: $417.99

CHAPTER 25

Red Oak is cradled in a valley between two hogback ridges, ancient mountains worn to large hills by receding glaciers. Pine covered, they so closely resemble Mississippi it was no wonder that Choctaw Scouts chose it as the location of the final destination for the tribe during removal. The Chahta almost flourished in the first thirty years after removal. They had traveled through hell to arrive in the new lands, only to have hell return during the war among the states. For the next thirty years, the Choctaw were under perpetual assault. The green of the hills filled with brush, bramble, and briar, and hid the texture of the earth. The brush must have also hid the boundary markers set by the tribe, the white granite obelisks set along the borders. By now they must have absorbed mold and easily blended into the forest floor, much like the Choctaw—there, but hidden and obscured by Boomer land lust.

Eben is a clerk for the Choctaw Treasury Department during the zenith of the polity for the rattlesnake people. Shorthanded as the department is, he is formally an Inspector but really he is the Clerk/Lead Investigator/English to Choctaw Translator/Roustabout and Gopher, with all duties well-blended together. If they were ingredients for stew, they would mix into a brownish color looking remarkably like *halafa*. When he wasn't tired from reading stacks of papers on his desk he is reclining on his side with his saddle-sore butt not touching anything. The Morgan case caused pain to radiate from his coccyx like spasms after diarrhea. He had more saddle contact abrasions from that case then he cared to remember.

Isom James subtly jabs, "Your ol buddy Mac was out here yesterday."

Eben responds, "Your best friend?"

"Naw, my friend has a good-looking wife who sorta looks like mine."

"I bet your best friend worries that his wife won't stop being bossy."

"I won't tell Evie you said that about Exia, you tit-whipped mangy dog. By the by, if ya'll would quit spendin' all that money in court you could afford to hire me some help insteada bringin' virgins like yourself out into the field." Isom's chest moves up and down from his restrained laughter.

"Isom, if you were half the Lighthorseman your daddy was, you woulda already had Mac tied to a tree with thirteen lashes across his back."

"If I was my daddy, I woulda already kicked you in the ass for dragging me out here to watch white folk peckin' the dirt like chickens. You know I can't arrest if I know he ain't Indian. That last boy I drug wounded to Tushkahoma turned out not to be a half-breed," he said with a laugh. "He was leakin out his leg though."

While Isom laughs, Eben strains to make out the activity below. "I don't know how Mac made it back from DC already. Parker shoulda locked him up for stealing cows rather than that trespass charge."

"He already been before the ol Billy Goat?!"

"Yeah, apparently he was joined at the hip with ol' Payne and those others out promoting the opening of the strip."

"Who told you this?"

"When we filed on the Red River case Morgan was listed as a surveyor for the company and he also was listed as one for the Pine Oak Coal Company. It turns out he was working for the Commissioner of Indian Affairs, out scouting mineral deposits to ensure that his buddies got access to the mineral rights first. Since the Commissioner was appointed by McKinley he was able to make sure that all mineral surveys conducted by the Department of the Interior crossed his desk. I know this because when Morgan was brought before Parker he tried to use his being an agent for the Commissioner as limiting his "culpability," a white word that means "guilt." Of course there was no direct memo assigning Mac as an agent of the Department of Interior that I could locate. He was taken in with those other Boomers for trespassing and the legal wizard Parker wanted to gavel him into prison, but those railroad attorneys won over the jury. The main attorney was a guy called Skinner."

"The Commissioner getting some of that gravy from the tribe then?" Isom stares at the activity in the valley as rail cars are being connected.

"The Commissioner's son is the principal owner of the Red River Coal Company." Eben counts the rail cars but the clearing ends right where the tree line occludes the back end of the train from direct vision.

"So what you're sayin' is my money for a deputy is down there?" Isom gently ribs his horse to walk, beginning the descent through a path walked frequently enough to be devoid of briars.

"I wish we could beat it out of him, it'd be easier than court!" Eben turns his horse to follow.

"I got my hickory axe handle with me, you want me to break anything in particular?" Isom moves the reins to his mouth and pulls his metal star from a breast-pocket fastening it to his shirt.

Eben follows about ten feet back, watching Isom's horse as it lumbers hoof over hoof, trying not to stumble downhill on the gravel path. The path forward provides plentiful opportunities for daydreaming, and scenarios cascade past his imagination; would he yell like he wanted to at Mac and get rowdy? Would he tell Isom to take Mac down like he is tempted to? He could see in his mind's eye Isom hitting Mac below the knees. In the fantasy he could put his boot on Mac's throat. In each scenario, Mac would confess to everything and beg not to be dragged before Parker. Fantasy of justice makes the loss in the game more bitter.

The images in his mind and reality are always far apart, and then Eben realizes he is in his wagon in 1910. The present comes back into focus while he is rocking, the wheels rolling through the ruts, and the horse's rump rhythmically flexing side to side. His emotions are high leaving Muskogee, and his memory has fused with the present, following the ruts gouged in his heart. The enemy never really changes, the same malevolence flowing from incident to incident. Eben fantasizes about what he could imagine Isom would do now, twenty years later. He would ride up to Judge Skinner's office, pull out his Winchester, push shells into the chamber, and cock the lever.

Eben fantasizes about doing his job Isom's way with a flying axe handle; maybe Exia would wait for him to get out of prison? Maybe he could live the fugitive life back in the woods? What would it matter? He could cut the head off of the snake Skinner and there would be a dozen ready to slither into his den, most likely the Attorney Smith.

There are no heroes like Isom anymore. Eben thinks back and whispers to himself, "Was Isom shot a year later or nine months?" Isom had cornered some bootleggers out near Robbers Cave accidentally when he was seeking to serve a warrant for a horse theft by a Choctaw from Kinta. He startled the bootleggers who assumed he came for them and bullets flew, striking him down.

The day Isom fell was one of the saddest Eben could remember. Exia could barely console Evie. Their ten-year-old daughter, Rhoda, had lapsed into shock, screaming as she saw her lifeless daddy's head bouncing on the back of the wagon. Eben was outside with Isom's brothers and cousins constructing the casket. One brother was sawing slats, measuring with string according to the dimensions taken from Isom's body. One nails the bottom slat and another younger brother nails the side boards to the foot boards, all of them active and somber, preparing the small ark for the flood of emotion later that day. Inside the house is filled with mourning as Evie's cousins cook for the gathering family. Evie and her sisters pull off the blood-soaked clothing to prepare the body for bathing. Evie screams seeing the bullet wound in his chest and Eben rushes in to see Exia cradling her on the floor. The other women began bathing his body, all the while singing Choctaw hymns about resurrection, their melody saturated with sorrow.

More than a friend had died that day; the father of his nephews and nieces. His sister-in-law was lost in despair for awhile and Exia stayed on for three weeks to bear her through the pain. Every time a protector is lost the encroachment of darkness tears at the canopy of peace. As he rides in the wagon Eben wonders if the same fate awaits himself. You slap the bull and you will get the horn. He had tried to slap Morgan once before and lost. Now Morgan's pet dog is a judge.

CHAPTER 26

Gypsy Oil had been brought to the Oklahoma Supreme Court involving the oil funds of Thomas Gilcrease, an educated Muscogee Nation citizen. Gilcrease was lucky. Gypsy Oil was owned by Gulf Oil of Texas, one of the largest producers of the Cushing Oil Field. Gilcrease prevailed, which is not common for his Muscogee sisters and brothers. Gilcrease was educated and not an orphan. His allotment was south of Ida Glenn's where the famous Glenpool was discovered.

Gypsy was just one of so many oil companies. The companies changed titles faster than some actresses change husbands. Hill Oil & Gas would sell their company to Cosden Oil Company. McGee of Hill Oil & Gas would start another company known as Noon Oil & Gas. McMan Oil Company, owned by Chapman and McFarlin, would sell their company to Cosden as well. Though Montfort Jones sold his shares to Prairie Oil, he then changed his fealty to Chapman. The knights of the oil table shift allegiance and flags faster than most could understand.

Cosden had built an independent refinery in Tulsa. Luckily the Sherman Anti-trust Act had disabled Standard Oil from Rockefeller's hostile takeover of Tulsa. So the knights of four realms had combined to fight. It wasn't the War of the Roses, more like War of the Briars.

Cosden needed capital to create his mergers. He got his funding from Wall Street and a financier known as C. J. Stralem. Stralem had the financial backing because he represented Atlantic & Gulf Petroleum. Atlantic was one of the Standard Oil companies that Rockefeller maintained shares in even after so many of his companies were broken up. Rockefeller, the son of a con man, had, in essence, won.

Cosden would rename his company Mid-Continent Oil. Mid-Continent Oil would become Sun Oil Company, the owner of the Tulsa Refinery. There is a beautiful Art Deco building in downtown Tulsa that is known as the Cosden building. Somewhere someone keeps writing Ullie on its façade.

There was never an investigation into who hanged Ullie and Hanna. But the Knights of the Oklahoma judiciary would manage to hire more Knights to save the corpse of the damsel in distress; the Dead Indian Act meant that the Knights in shining armor still retained their cause though their damsel was beyond distraught. John B. Meserve would be appointed special master to conduct fact finding on the Ullie Eagle oil case. He had to wrangle over fifty attorneys who were representing over two hundred Muscogee people who were suddenly relatives of Ullie's. Four of the attorneys were Joseph A. Gill, N.A. Gibson, Charles Rogers, and Creekmore Wallace. It could be argued that orphan funds built Tulsa. How many Oklahoma lawyers fight tribes while using law books purchased from the proceeds of injustice?

On December 23, 1929, the 10th Circuit Court of Appeal finally hears another appeal in Fish v. Kennamer the District Judge. The appeal was also against Circuit Judges Lewis, Cotteral, and Phillips. So many judges in an appeal. It reads,

> ¶1 These are applications for writs of mandamus to compel the District Judge to make certain orders in a cause pending before him. The litigation in which the orders are sought is over an allotment of 160 acres of land in Creek County, Oklahoma, to Ullie Eagle, a full-blood Creek Indian who died intestate and without issue in June, 1902. In 1923, Harriett Hosey, with several other Indians who joined her as plaintiffs, brought an action of ejectment in the State district court of Creek County for said 160 acres and for the rents, royalties, and profits taken from said land by the named defendants and for damages, all in the sum of $25,000,000.
>
> [The Creek County courthouse is in Sapulpa. Attorney's McGee and Jackson have law offices in Sapulpa]
>
> They alleged that Ullie Eagle died intestate and without issue, leaving surviving her no father, mother, sister, or brother, but left as her sole and only heir-at-law one Patience DePriest, who is enrolled as a Creek citizen, that said Patience DePriest was the daughter of one Jane Strickland, Jane Strickland was the sister of one Sealie, Sealie was the mother of one Tochee, and Tochee was the mother of Ullie Eagle; that said Tochee, mother, and Sealie, grandmother, of Ullie, and Jane Strickland, sister of Sealie, all died prior to the death of Ullie Eagle, and said Patience DePriest

was the next of kin and sole heir of said Ullie Eagle, and that said Patience DePriest died in September, 1904, and left as her sole surviving heirs-at-law, the plaintiff Harriett Hosey and her coplaintiffs. Several oil companies and several individuals were made defendants, who it appears claimed title, or some interest, as owners or lessees, mediately or immediately, under conveyance made by Nellie Fish, who, they claim, was the nearest relation to Ullie Eagle at the time of her death, within the meaning of the Creek law of descent and distribution, and was her sole surviving heir. Soon after this suit was instituted several other Indians, known as the Guthrie group, were permitted to intervene as plaintiffs, they also claiming to be heirs of Ullie Eagle. Harriett Hosey and her co-plaintiffs admitted the claim of the Guthrie group. Then the Malone group, who claimed to be heirs were admitted. Then the Monahwee group of claimants were permitted to intervene. The two last-named groups claimed heirship through a different ascending-descending line from the original plaintiffs and the Guthrie group. No objection was made to the intervention of said three groups. The two last-named groups joined issue with the original plaintiffs and set up their own claims as sole heirs. After answers were filed the case went to trial before a jury in the State court and the plaintiffs had a verdict. A motion for new trial was sustained. Thereupon other groups of Indian claimants asserting to be heirs of Ullie Eagle were admitted as parties, some while the action was pending in the State court, and some after it was removed to the Federal court, in the manner hereinafter stated, until there were in all some nineteen different groups of Indians, consisting of about two hundred persons in all, and all claiming to be collateral kindred. These interveners joined issue between themselves as to heirship and with the original plaintiffs. The case was removed to the Federal court pursuant to Act of April 12, 1926 (44 Stat. 239). After removal, the Federal court permitted some of the groups referred to above to intervene as parties under claims of heirship. Some of the defendants filed crossbills and joined therein a number of Indians who had not intervened but who, the crossbills alleged, were asserting claims to the allotment. Under the State practice the privilege of intervention is broad, permitting, it seems, everyone who claims an interest in the subject matter involved to come into a case, and apparently no serious objection was raised to that procedure until removal to the Federal court. The plaintiffs and some of the other groups moved that the cause be remanded to the State court, and that being overruled, the original plaintiffs and some of the interveners moved that all equitable defenses and cross-bills be stricken out, that interventions of different groups which had been permitted by the Federal court be also vacated, and repeated attacks of that kind were made throughout the progress of the case in the Federal court. The gravamen of the insistence here by these petitioners for the writ is based on the contention that the action of the original plaintiffs and the Guthrie group who joined with them as plaintiffs, was in ejectment, a plain-and-simple action at law, in which they were entitled to trial by jury without interference from all others who were claiming adversely to them. The court below denied all of these contentions and over opposition of petitioners here transferred the equity issues in the cause to the equity docket and appointed a master to take the proof and report his findings of fact and conclusions of law. Among other exhibits showing the course of procedure counsel have submitted to us the report of the master, who found as a fact "that at the time of the death of Ullie Eagle on June 8, 1902, she left surviving her as her nearest relation Nellie Fish, her aunt." He further found that none of the intervening groups, nor the original plaintiffs, had sustained their claims to heirship.

¶7 It would be a travesty of justice to say that equity is powerless to protect one in possession of lands purchased in good faith against nineteen sets of claimants of the title, but that he must stand by and wait until each set sues him in turn and take the chances of contradictory verdicts of juries on facts which, under the obvious circumstances of this case, are difficult of correct ascertainment in such trials. Mr. Justice Harlan, while presiding on the circuit, said this in Sheldon et al. v. Keokuk Northern Line Packet Co. et al. (C.C.) 8 F. 769, 770: "It has been held, by the supreme court of the United States, to be impracticable to lay down any fixed, unbending rule as to what constitutes multifariousness or misjoinder of causes of action. Oliver v. Piatt, 3 How. 411 [11 L. Ed. 622]; Gaines v. Chew, 2 How. 619 [11 L. Ed. 402]; Barney v. Latham [103 U.S. 205, 26 L. Ed. 514], October term, 1880–1. The court must necessarily exercise a large, though, of course, a sound discretion in allowing the union in the same suit of matters which do not alike or equally affect all the parties. Each case must depend upon its special circumstances, and the necessities which may arise out of the due administration of justice in that case. As a general rule, the court will not compel parties to incur the expense, vexation, and delay of several suits, where the transactions constituting the subject of the litigation, or out of which

> the litigation arises, are so connected by their circumstances as to render it proper and convenient that they should be examined in the same suit, and full relief given by one comprehensive decree. A different rule would often prove to be both oppressive and mischievous, and could result in no possible benefit to any litigant whose object was not simply to harass his adversary, but to ascertain what were his just legal rights. As to the general propositions there can be no doubt under the authorities."
>
> ¶10 For the reasons stated the writ will be denied in both of these applications. It is so ordered.

The claims of Patience DePriest are ironic. Had the court just examined the Muscogee Creek Nation's Dawes census card 906, conducted at Checotah, they would have seen there is not a link given between Jenni Strickland, who is Artussee, and Sealie, whose mother is listed as Tinfalagee in Dawes census 1357, conducted at Tuskegee.

CHAPTER 27

If Sherlock Holmes was summoned to investigate the death of Ullie in 1902, where would he begin? "Once you eliminate the impossible, whatever remains, no matter how improbable, must be the truth."

Ullie was enrolled by the Dawes Commission on March 13, 1902. Ullie and her cousin Hanna were found hanged June 8, 1902. Their death coincides with the "Dead Indian Act." Ullie's allotment was worth $26,000,000 eventually because of mineral lease #24200. Ullie's allotment was over thirty miles from Sealie's. Ullie probably never even saw the land. The property is two miles past Shamrock, going towards Drumright, where the large Cushing Oil Field begins. Wells are still pumping today. Maybe someone approached Sealie with an offer to drill Ullie's land. Ullie's grandmother was ninety years old and probably would not give any white man the right to Ullie's property; supposition based on Sealie's experience with white men and being a survivor of distinct historical trauma caused by removal would suggest that. Ullie is not the only orphan killed for land or money, but maybe she was one of the first, the canary in a cage.

In 1898, the federal government only deployed eight Indian Police to patrol the entire Muscogee Nation. They were each only paid $10 a month as a salary and expenses. Prior to the federal takeover, federal officers received mileage and payment for submitting warrants. Pine Ridge reservation had over seventy Indian Police. There were forty-four Queendoms in the Muscogee confederacy and thus there were forty-four Lighthorsemen who were the police of the Muscogee Nation. There would have been a Lighthorseman for Artussee and Nuyaka. There would have been an investigation had the Muscogee retained their government. If the Federal Indian Police patrol reported on the hanging then that would be in archives, possibly.

Who hanged eight-year-old Ullie and her cousin Hanna?

In 1898, when the federal government had the lands surveyed there was one surveyor, one rodman, one moundman, two axmen, one camp teamster, and one cook. The entire party eventually totaled eighteen men in the field. Their names are not listed in the employees for Indian Agency Service for 1898. If any person knew where oil seepage was occurring it would have been one of them. They would have known the Township, Range, and Section as well as anyone. If any of their names were on a lease prior to #24200 then the culprits could be examined for crimes in other states.

Did any of the survey party kill Ullie and Hanna?

In 1902, the farmers who had "improvements" on allottee lands filed complaints with the Union Agency. In the Union Agency report it was noted on page 202 by J. Shoenfelt that the "allotments of minors were being taken possession of by unscrupulous persons claiming to have rented or purchased them from the allottees or someone claiming to represent them." If the agricultural lease for Ullie's allotment recorded their name then they might have a monetary motive.

Did some farmer with an illegal agriculture lease kill Ullie and Hanna?

In December 1896, Albert P. McBride and Camden Bloom were the first to drill at the Red Fork. They drilled a dry hole and then went to work for Cudahy Oil to drill the Nellie Johnstone.

The Nellie Johnstone well was discovered because of a green-black seepage in a water well and was subsequently drilled in 1897 creating an early oil boom around Bartlesville. The federal government shut down leases until a law could be drafted on how mineral leases were to be conducted. In 1904, two oil pioneers arrived in Bartlesville, the Phillips, and they would eventually control the town. Technically the Johnstone lease was not legal. The lands had not officially been surveyed yet. Wildcatters had no compunction about violating the law.

Did McBride and Bloom drill the wells on Ullie's allotment? Were they responsible for Ullie and Hanna's death?

Early in 1901, two Pennsylvania oil developers, John S. Wick and Jesse A. Heydrick, got a dubious lease on 410,000 acres in the Creek Nation and they focused on land near Sapulpa. Any allotee lease required approval of the Commissioner of Indian Affairs as set out in regulation in 1898. Each lease required two witnesses for each signature and a Surety Bond. In addition the lease could not exceed five years. Technically no one was allowed leases of that size. The train company would not accept a note as payment for the drilling equipment from Wick and Heydrick. Two local doctors, John C. W. Bland and Fred S. Clinton, bailed them out. In return, they agreed to drill the well on the allotment of Sue A. Bland, wife of Dr. Bland, at Red Fork. The doctors had likely been recruited to the Muscogee Nation following a smallpox outbreak in April 1899. Red Fork touched off the Oil boom in Tulsa when, on June 24, 1901, the well shot oil thirty feet over the derrick. Sue Bland's allotment technically is Red Fork and located at Township 19, Range 12 East, and Section 22. Allotments directly east of Bland include Fred S. Clinton's in Section 23. Allotments throughout Section 22 and all of the T19 R12 include at least five Perrymans.

Did Wick and Heydrick drill the well on Ullie's allotment? Were they responsible for Ullie and Hanna's death?

The Chief of the Muscogee people in 1901 was Pleasant Porter. Chief Porter's mother was a mixed-blood Creek, the daughter of Tahlopee Tustunnuggee and Lydia Perryman. Chief Porter's family cemetery is located at Leonard which is southeast of Bixby. Did he sign the lease with Wick and Heydrick? Was he related in any way to Sue A. Bland? Lewis Perryman, Bell Perryman, Hector Perryman, Douglas Perryman, and Jenneha Perryman have allotments surrounding Mrs. Bland. Was she a Perryman?

If she was a relative, did the Chief let the foxes in the henhouse? Does he share a portion of the blame for Ullie and Hanna being murdered? Probably not, but he did allow a huge illegal lease of Muscogee territory. Did the acreage include Ullie's allotment?

The Dawes Commisioners in 1897 had a yearly salary of $5,000, or $145,000 in today's money. Archibald McKennon, Senator Henry L. Dawes, Frank Armstrong, Alexander Montgomery, and Tams Bixby were the Commission. They were well remunerated.

In hearings conducted April 22, 1904, Representative Lind of Minnesota debated a report that exposed corruption in the Dawes Commission. Tams Bixby, the Chairman of the Dawes Commission, J. George Wright, Indian Inspector, and C. R. Breckinridge, a member of the Dawes Commission, were called before the House of Representatives. In 1903, the three had created the Canadian Valley Trust Company. The company was already buying up real estate in several towns that had been surveyed. All the men got very rich before statehood.

Representative Lind stated, "The men sent as guardians to the Indian population of the Indian territory, sent there to protect the Indians, instead of doing so have organized themselves into various corporate schemes for the purpose, as is here charged of looting their wards, of profiting from their positions, of speculation in their official duties."

Tams Bixby was the Chairman of the Republican Committee for Oklahoma Statehood.

Did Tams Bixby allot the land to Ullie personally? Tams was corrupt and no doubt he helped generate the momentum of children being killed for minerals, but finding his links would be a monumental undertaking.

It is far less likely, but while any of the large oil companies involved in the Ullie case could have motives it becomes difficult to map what they could have been. No doubt any of the land men hired by the companies could have been ruthless. It wouldn't matter, the upper executives would have found ways to insulate their culpability. The first non-Muscogee listed on Ullie's property in Township 17 has the Grantor named as Katie Bear and the Grantee named A. H. Purdy. Another Muscogee allottee named Wesley Sawyer is noted as the Grantor, and the Grantee is Hill Oil & Gas. Did A. H. Purdy work for Hill Oil & Gas?

Was A. H. Purdy a landman for Hill Oil & Gas? Was A. H. Purdy somehow responsible for the deaths of Ullie and Hanna? The first snout in the trough is significant.

An S. J. Scott is listed as a Grantor and the Grantee is listed as Montfort Jones. Bermont Oil Company entered the scene on Ullie's allotment.

There is no doubt that McMan Oil was born and swam in the most corrupt town in Oklahoma during the booms: Holdenville. McMan Oil held the #24200 mineral lease with Ullie's Aunt Nellie. How did they get ahold of the lease? Since Rogers and Jackson were VPs of the Tulsa Bank, and Jackson practiced law in Sapulpa where the court is, did they have a land man? In Oklahoma, no one from the public is allowed to view the guardianship records in court houses without a judge's order; the state passed laws protecting the privacy of the ward, or, more likely, the guardian. Did Rep. Rogers write that law?

Nowata County would have originally been under the protection of the Cherokee Nation's Cooweescoowee District. It would have become Lenahpa County in the Indian state of Sequoyah.

Okfuskee County would have originally been under the protection of the Muscogee Nation's Deep Fork District. It would have become Arbeka County in the Indian state of Sequoyah. In Okfuskee County, American Indian minors would be owed over $11,458,696.80 to buy food.

Eddie Wesley, a Muscogee orphan, was owed $2,000.00. In 1915, to rent a house for a middle-class family would cost $25 per month or $300 a year. Heat and day-to-day expenses were $18.50 a month for a family, or $222 a year. Eddie could have supported his own families.

NOWATA COUNTY

James A. Walker, Jr.

OKFUSKEE COUNTY

Minnie Fink, nee McKellopp

Roy McKinley Holmes

Luisa Wesley

Eddie Wesley: $2,000.00

Maudie Emarthlochee

Raymond Douglas

Sallie Scott

James Barnett: $20.00

Louisa Canard: $40.00

May Etta Cox

Fannie Ann Ditzler

Taylor Low: $60.00

Annie Garrett

Harvey Davis

Nicie Goobes: $30.00

Robert Halloway

Lena Harjochee

Polly Harjo: $305.79

James Harjo

Jonas Harjo: $500.00

Joseph Harjo

Jimmie Harjoche

Harper Harjoche

Martha Harjoche

Lottie Harjoche

Adam Harjoche

Mable Harjo: $1,030.00

Joe Harjo

Willie Hen: $1,000.00

Albertha Jennings: $400.00

Maddie Johnson: $500.00

Edmond Lewis

Lano McKellop: $100.00

Barnogee Parnosky

Josiah Randolph: $1,361.60

India Roberts

Hattie Simmer

Lucinda Simmer

Pete Simmer

Dave Watson

Julia Henderson: $77.26

Eddie Watson: $225.00

Peter Johnson

Noah Johnson: $1,584.01

Houston Hill: $213.18

Lester Knight: $1,629.55

Mallev Ahfonoke: $1,231.44

Stella Stoddard: $86.15

Mamie Stoddard: $136.05

Joseph Stoddard: $57.20

Gennellie King: $916.65

Gennellie King: $200.00

Gennellie King: $700.00

Gennellie King

Fred Vann: $800.00

James Samuel: $1,361.60

Sallie Lowe: $225.00

Jimmie Yaholar: $35.00

Louis Wesley: $154.45

Ada Wesley: $500.00

Ada Wesley: $720.00

Lessey Yarhola

Rhoda Tiger

Nora Watson: $77.65

Alvin Collins: $2,020.00

Gladys Rylee

Larty Fields: $1,748.70

Israel Long: $1,350.00

Leola Barnett: $200.00

Leola Barnett

Robert Knight: $2,056.44

Sadie Yahola: $100.00

Malinda Foster: $100.00

Cora Foster: $1,404.06

William Foster: $1,420.35

Lula Foster: $40.00

Molly Ann Harjo: $1,723.53

Raymond R. Douglas: $200.00

Raymond R. Douglas

Raymond R. Douglas

Lizzie Johnson

Sandy Johnson

Lizzie Johnson: $400.00

William Arpoika

Lena Hennehuchee: $3,857.94

Bertha Cole: $1,000.00

Willie Cole: $651.95

Willie Cole2: $275.00

Willie Cole3: $1,000.00

Bertha Cole

Sampson Tecumseh: $56.22

Carolina Tecumseh: $597.65

Carolina Tecumseh

Georgina Smith: $250.00

Lucy Harjo: $30.00

George Sullivan

George Sullivan2: $1,432.01

Ida Goodner

Maggie Golgler

Floyd Williams

Lina McCoy: $130.00

Elizabeth Barnett: $300.00

Arthur Holmes: $160.00

Ellie Holmes: $160.00

Simer Coon: $1,910.00

Lewis Shelton: $800.00

Leola Shelton: $1,312.00

Katie Johnson: $1,800.00

Katie Johnson: $420.00

Amos Iimboy: $574.27

Jesse Knight: $244.57

Martha Yahola: $76.09

George Robinson: $1,100.00

Nelson Robinson: $300.00

Louisa Robinson: $1,000.00

Mable Hale: $997.42

Causey Dan: $171.15

Edmond Dunson: $718.25

Lizzie Mackey et al

Dave Jefley: $22.08

Tommy Hopson: $800.00

Ida Watson Barnett: $26.51

Ida Watson Barnett: $16.80

Billie Barnett

James Harjo

Jonas Harjo: $320.00

Joseph Harjo

Willie Hen: $1,900.00

Albert Sands: $300.73

Leah Frank: $236.68

Kogee Simmer

Kogee Simmer2: $830.00

Jackson Hill: $1,735–53

Sam Davis: $750.00

Sam Davis2: $242.00

Legus Fields: $260.00

Bessie Fields: $210.00

Emma Berryhill: $110.60

Anderson Berryhill: $345.56

John Berryhill: $45.55

Chenowee Johnson: $265.81

Echoluste Brown

Cornelius Nail: $1.70

Cornelius Nail2

Cornelius Nail3

Robinson Foster: $1,642.32

Guy Smith: $579.50

Addie Smit: $24.00

Fannie Smith: $80.00

Lena Johnson

Ultis Johnson

Mersaly Johnson

Bessie Johnson: $390.40

Dorothea Bowlegs: $103.72

Isaac Deere: $1,089.00

Isaac Deere2

Taylor Johnson: $1,175.00

Minnie Deer: $261.52

John Beaver: $1,517.13

Arch Simmer

Mollie Taylor

Mollie Taylor2

Lilla Taylor $400.00

Sarho Sexer Harjo

Lucinda Fixico: $2,575.50

Lucinda Fixico: $1,200.00

Edmond Lewis: $110.00

Eddie Lewis: $64.35

Mosey Lewis: $108.75

Lillie Lewis: $76.05

Losanna West: $5,000.00

Mollie Taylor: $400.00

Phillip Johnson: $160.00

Phillip Johnson: $500.00

Quash Johnson: $150.00

Mattie Johnson: $160.00

Dave Yargee: $408.33

Isaac Johnson

Eddi Jimboy: $307.77

Lizzie Jimboy: $296.31

Amanda Jimboy: $691.07

Eddie Wesley: $1,768.01

Eddie Wesley2: $1,034.06

Eddie Wesley

Eddie Wesley $300.00

Louisa Wesley: $1,611.81

Louisa Wesley: $877.86

Louisa Wesley

Louisa Wesley

Thomas Holmes: $2,200.00

Dora Watson: $280.58

William Watson: $258.08

Lena Watson: $280.58

Bethel Watson: $285.98

Mary Ann Watson: $280.58

Sarna Fixico: $1,045.10

Hennehochee Fixico: $1,044.00

Earnest Mcintosh

Ernest Mcintosh2: $2,400.00

Earnest Mcintosh: $3,205.00

Wilford Mcintosh: $2,000.00

Wilford Mcintosh: $2,460.00

Samuel Simmer

Scott Simons: $747.09

Jennie Carter

Susie Carter: $310.00

Edward Harjo

Millissie Kannard: $232.11

Barnogee Parnosky: $1,600.00

Barnogee Parnosky: $133.80

Ellen Deer: $748.67

Arline Robinson: $337.30

Nellie Fixico: $328.42

Melisa Thompson: $2,539.51

Roy Franks: $60.50

Cora Harris: $300.00

Rena Holmes

George Johnson

Mariah Johnson: $80.00

George Johnson

Mariah Johnson

George Johnson: $700.00

Mariah Johnson: $720.00

Mariah Johnson: $700.00

George Johnson; $640.00

Louis Fisher: $102.80

Johnny Garrett

Monroe Moses: $1,000.00

Clinton Moses

Susan Moses

Susan Moses case: $489.80

Charlie McDermott

Lizzie McDermott: $86.71

Addie Bunner: $747.00

James W. Callahan: $254.50

Tommv Bruner: $1,500.00

John L. Hopwood: $612.50

Ira H. Hopwood

Ora P. Hopwood: $835.00

Jimmie Walker: $239.15

Jackson Laslev: $114.05

Midoge Tiger: $124.45

Seliva Tiger: $99.24

Annie Martin: $73.64

Sallie Deer McGirt: $426.30

Sallie McGirt: $358.33

Lela Dixon

Ralph Heneha: $70.00

Roy Heneha: $231.00

Ilba Fixico: $166.07

Malinda Bird: $574.77

Willie Bird

Jacob Fife :$395.50

Sandie Grayson: $550.00

Arney Hill

Peggy Hill: $500.00

Frank Carolina: $300.00

Ed Carolina

Suiter Fixico: $410.00

Nora Harjo: $23.33

Leona Harjo: $23.31

Jessie Hario: $23.33

Lois Henderson: $80.00

Loise Henderson: $80.00

Landy McGirt: $163.50

Wesley Scott: $440.38

Nelson Durant

William Durant: $800.00

Emma West: $866.93

Wash Cawrnev

Josie Bear: $1,055.62

Henry Samuels: $300.00

Almon Sawyer: $200.80

Noami Inman: $430.00

Lizzie West: $283.40

Albertha Jennings

Carrie Lee Henderson: $126.67

Bular Henderson: $126.67

James F. Henderson: $126.67

Victory Henderson: $126.67

Eddie Henderson: $126.67

Azell Carolina: $220.00

Rosevelt Gilbert: $1,010.00

John Henry Gibbs: $10.00

Corain Gibbs: $265.50

Maria Sango

Nancy D. Collins: $1,800.00

Hettie Brown: $300.00

John Watson: $34.50

Thomas Watson: $27.00

Stella Watson: $27.00

Louisa Watson: $40.00

Hettie Brown: $360.00

Leora Johnson

Elnora Willis

Elnora Willis: $900.00

Edward Wallace: $300.00

Albert Jennings

Albertha Jennings: $1,600.00

Mabel Harjo

Davis Bruner

Bennie Hawkins

David Bruner

Bennie Hawkins: $500.00

Davis Bruner: $1,470.00

Johnnie Cobb: $275.10

Edward Bruner: $4,398.00

Johnnie Cobb: $260.00

Billy Bruner: $2,625.91

Johnnie Cobb: $250.00

Edward Bruner: $2,705.00

Amos Harjochee

Billy Bruner: $2,000.00

Ida Wells: $320.00

Robert Hicks: $378.00

Janette Knight: $444.57

London Knight: $782.98

Walter Knight: $404.57

Rena Holmes: $274.00

Rhoda Hill: $400.00

John Bruner: $200.00

Rhoda Hill

Lee Etta Bruner: $383.41

Willie Moore: $1,000.00

Ida Bruner: $500.00

Mary Williams: $350.00

Gibson Coker: $100.00

Mary Williams: $127. 52

Gibson Coker: $150.00

Henry Vincent: $145.00

Alfred Deer: $414.21

Miller Tiger

Minnie Deer: $414.21

Hettie Tiger

Josiah Deer: $374.21

Jefferson Tiger

William Self

Wilson Tiger

Maggie O. Self

Roxanna Williams nee Homes: $500.00

Gallie R. Self

Gallie R. Self

Roxanna Williams nee Homes: $550.00

Maggie Ophelia Self

Chemarye: $40.00

James Olden

John Brown: $656.00

Grather Olden: $400.00

Mary Reed

James Olden: $1,600.00

Elrie Lampkin: $200.00

Grather Olden

Lula Foster: $24.00

Bennie Coleman

Henry Foster: $24.00

Maggie Coleman

Olean Lumpkins: $60.00

Opal Coleman

Edmond Hardridge: $1,060.00

Lena Harjoche

Thomas Robinson

Jimmie Harjoche: $40.00

Lilly Davis

Jimmie Harjoche

Sylvia Brooks

Harper Harjoche

Laura Brooks

Martha Harjoche

Louie Barnett

Lottie Harjoche

Albert Mitchell

Adam Harjoche

Louie Barnett: $40.00

Joe Harjo

Albert Mitchell

George C. Foster

Albert Lewis

Katie Brown

Albert Lewis: $440.00

Sarne Bullet

Jimmie Willis: $640.00

Dave Watson

Julia Willis: $1,505.00

Hulley Barnett

Elnora Barnett: $3,546.00

Robert Walker

Abraham Lincoln Patrick

Martha Carr

Abraham Lincoln Patrick

Israel Wade

Maudie Emorthloches $378.50

Colbert Coker

Colbert Coker: $960.00

Colbert Coker

Jennetta Sango: $1,100.00

Julia Hart: $1,000.00

Julia Hart

Flossie Williams

Janie Holmes

Pearlie Holmes

Raymond Holmes

Angie Lugrand

Alfred Lugrand: $700.00

Mos Cudjo

Lee Cudjo

Feodo Cudjo

Nettie Harjo

CHAPTER 28

Morgan proclaims himself a "Pioneer" during the WPA's Pioneer Papers interviews in the 1930s. At the time, he is in the twilight of his years and has begun to reminisce on the good old days. He paints a picture of Columbus having discovered wild lands needing to be tamed, attempting to repair the image of his feral behavior.

He is among the first in the trough of public giveaways. His snout roots for oil, coal, nickel, or any other mineral that the BIA will grant after he squeals. He isn't unique as a former employee of railroads. Several of the former employees of the rail companies become successful after serving as Indian Agents and Dawes Clerks during the division of property known as the allotment. Indian lands are divided among tribal members so that a large amount of surplus can be given to the public domain. The lands are never contiguous among families to prevent any further communalism; no problem if you're Amish. A little irony not known by many is that former Indian Agents become very successful statesmen in the new state. They acquire thousands of acres and yet they are never suspected as being communal. Abscond with the property and procure the power. Funny how the town of Bixby, named for Dawes Agent Tams Bixby, sits next door to the Glenpool oilfield.

"The lease for the Pine-Oak Coal Company provides for uninterrupted access to their properties, and I, quite frankly, don't see how rail cars belonging to the Texas Louisiana can be hijacked by Indians"

Skinner is arrogant in demeanor at the Muskogee courthouse flanked by other suits. Skinner is about five feet ten inches tall, with blonde hair receding at the widow's peak, causing the sandy tone of the top hair to resemble a desolate island.

"I'm confident that the Choctaw Nation will return the property of Texas Louisiana in the near future," Agent Bryson responds, looking in the direction of Treasurer Battiest.

Battiest, in response, leans back to get an interpretation from Eben. Eben knows, however, that Battiest needs no interpreter and that he is using a strategy often employed during these type of meetings; slow down deliberation and try to control the direction of the agenda.

"I think Skinner knows that we have an idea of the amount of coal they've mined already from the way he's talking. He's too confident. He probably will file suit as soon as this hearing is complete, if he hasn't already. They will move to keep our evidence out by calling our action by the Lighthorse illegal."

Eben sits, face fixated on the table, an elongated and brown edifice with large, fat, scrolled legs. The Texas Louisiana Rail Company builds a document fortification in stacks to intimidate the the Indian agent and Choctaw agents; litigation will follow. The Texas Rail people consist of Attorney Skinner, Surveyor Morgan, and a young intern who is not named.

"We should find out their relationship to the coal company. If they're one and the same then we know the type of delays they will attempt legally. Maybe we can prevent this case from going there like the Red River one." As Battiest finishes he picks up a glass to sip water.

Eben thinks carefully on how to be succinct before speaking, "If the rail cars are yours then when did you contract with the Pine Oak Coal Company?

Skinner gently rolls his fingers on the table. "And you are an associate of the Choctaw Treasurer, I presume? You were introduced, but your title was not mentioned." As he speaks, the intern looks prepared to begin transcription.

Eben, amused, replies, "I am an Agent of the Choctaw Treasury."

"Well then, please assure Mr. Battiest that our company has many relationships and provides service to diverse clients. We like to think that we assist everyone and have enjoyed our relationship with your tribe as well. Now previous Treasury agents as yourselves had developed a cordial relationship with our company and I am sure that a mutual understanding can be achieved." Skinner sits quietly, expression blank, after finishing his proposal.

Agent Bryson, beaming from the rhetorical volley, decides to assist Skinner. Ever the Dawes Clerk, Agent Bryson is suited in a shirt that is browning from sweat around the collar and has a very friendly face that could allay any fears while reading tribal obituaries. "That's what the interest of the Bureau is. To find some common ground to negotiate a mutually beneficial solution for the Choctaw Nation and the Texas Louisiana. If I might add, I do not believe the tribe has the requisite jurisdiction to detain rail cars. I hope an incident can be alleviated. I shudder to think that your Lighthorsemen or employees of Texas Louisiana would suffer any injuries because of a misunderstanding. If there had been citizens of the United States on those cars it would have generated much controversy, and I fear troops would have been called up to ensure the peace. After all the problems the Bureau has had while conducting the census among the Creeks and some factions of the Cherokee, as well as your tribe, we have attempted to anticipate any future dilemmas. We hope to avoid them at all costs if possible."

Eben translates to Battiest, "This guy has probably gotten his family a free trip back east on the iron road. He's in their pocket isn't he?" Battiest nods, then gulps. Eben continues: "I may have gambled too much on having Isom, Reuben, and Kanatabby seize those cars. I thought we could smoke out Pine-Oak easier than this, but it sounds like they got this agent primed to threaten a shootout on their behalf."

Battiest relaxes slightly in the chair, "Look at their faces, they don't want a shootout. They know we have made the connection on the Red River case back to the Indian Commissioner's boy. They may be worried that we'll get all native on them, which would disrupt their acquisitions. They also know that the Nation has filed charges against Postoak for accepting bribes and he sang against Texas Louisiana after he found his white allies not providing for his legal defense."

"Treasurer Battiest has assured me to state that we do not desire any fight, but that we have a legal right to require a full payment of royalties owed to the Choctaw Nation. We did not understand that the cars were the property of the Texas Louisiana at the time of our stopping them from leaving the Red Oak area. All we knew is that we had a company taking minerals from land still owned by a citizen of the Choctaw Nation, and under Choctaw law, as you know, the Nation is still the guardian of our interest." Eben reclines away from the table knowing that the "ignorant" full-blood ruse may have worked for Battiest here, but it will not work in smoking out the full details from Postoak, who is skilled in Choctaw maneuvers. Eben knows that Postoak probably isn't even aware of the full scheme during the leases anyways and tying him to Pine-Oak would not happen if the BIA is already on the side of Texas Louisiana. The most they could get is a corrupt Choctaw, but none of his puppet masters.

"So we can assume that the Choctaw Nation will be surrendering our Rail Cars back to us in the immediate future?" Skinner asks, face filled with chagrin.

Eben translates again, "Should we make them dump the coal?"

"It won't hurt to require that, but they won't," Battiest looks at the legs of the table, obviously captivated by the carvings, looking the silly primitive.

"We feel the coal should be removed from the cars until a formal lease has been executed with the Choctaw Nation; under BIA supervision of course," Eben, with diplomatic voice, almost gags from sweetness.

Skinner, not buying it, responds tersely, "Though I do not represent the Pine-Oak Company, who will ensure that their interest is represented in this process?"

"The Bureau has already begun corresponding with the principals of that company," Agent Bryson chimed in.

"I had written correspondence to you as the attorney of record for the Pine-Oak Company in the past Mr. Skinner, and I assumed you still were." Eben tries not to bristle while accusing Mr. Skinner of a lie.

Skinner, ever smug, "I was an attorney for them before coming under the employ of Texas Louisiana. Of course I have no knowledge of the events that have led to this unfortunate misunderstanding and would have worked out the details with the Choctaw Nation. I mentioned that I have had a cordial relationship with the Choctaw Nation and still feel a kin with your proud people."

Morgan looks at Eben with a masked glare, apparently bemused by the entertainment. He has probably heard from Postoak about a young hothead who is coming after Red River and poking around about who knew a *Hatak Nahollo* (White man) named Morgan. Now the profile is probably complete for Morgan. Eben knows he has played his hand, exposing himself as the scout who is hunting corruption. Eben hopes he has not overplayed his hand.

CHAPTER 29

In 1907, Oklahoma became the first state to elect a woman to a major state office. She would be heralded in the state as "Saint Kate" and "Good Kate," but never Glinda; she had no wand. Saint Kate was Catholic in a Protestant state. Her witness was faithful and she did unto the least of his all she could do.

When the Oklahoma Enabling Act went through, all property matters transferred from federal hands to the state. The state promptly appointed forty county judges as the guardians of 60,000 native minors whose land values were $130,000,000, not counting the oil valuation exceeding $25,000,000. In today's value, that is over $8,691,800,000. Eight billion dollars were stolen from children. Today, there would be FBI investigations numbering in the thousands.

Good Kate began her investigations of these orphans' property now under her umbrella. All the new legislature had given her was one small office with one attorney. She managed to expose case after case. The worst she found was Judge J. T. Barnes who had appointed his attorney friends' guardian *ad litem* over 6,000 Choctaw minors who had never seen a dime.

Another case among the Creeks came from parents of a boy who disappeared from his home in Jenks. He was found in London, England. Kidnappings and murders dominated the early years of Oklahoma.

By 1912, Kate had over 18,000 ongoing investigations. In 1914, the state legislature moved to stop her by slashing her budget. She lost her few staff, reducing her to conduct her business on a bench in the basement of the state capitol building.

Okmulgee County would have originally been under the protection of the Muscogee Nation's Okmulgee, Deep Fork, and Muskogee Districts. It would have become portions of Okmulgee, Arbeka, and Muskogee counties in the Indian state of Sequoyah. In Okmulgee County, American Indian minors would be owed over $18,610,622.07 to buy food.

OKLAHOMA COUNTY

Galen Younger

Daniel L. McClinton

OKMULGEE COUNTY

Shomie Grayson

Mary Alexander: $2,665.00

Joseph L. Hawkins: $62.00

Charles Lee Mcintosh: $95.70

Lucy Bradford: $320.00

Lula Bradford: $80.00

Wiley King: $653.04

George Tiger

Addie Davis: $6.95

George Davis: $2,900.91

John R. Woods: $1,582.71

Sealey Alexander: $1,447.62

Ruth Brinton: $1,337.91

Beatrice Grayson: $13,000.00

Lena Gray

Hugh Henry, Jr.: $473.27

Hettie Henry: $12,633.45

Alex Alexander: $1,428.86

Ralph M. Woods: $1,091.96

Florence L. Woods: $160.00

Elza Atkins: $3.259.10

Nina Starr: $2,615.43

Katie Carruth: $1,139.16

Sammy Taylor: $493.73

Lizie Pinkey: $759.21

Ben Dave Mcintosh: $139.15

Johnson Harjo: $510.31

Eliza Kannard: $683.64

Cilia Kannard: $162.94

Louisa Harjo: $58,514.00

Yarner Sugar: $1,789.92

Eddie Sugar: $294.97

Ada Scott: $93.00

Fanny Grey

Jefferson M. Myers: $13,604.87

Minnie T. Myers: $6,045.26

Caesar King: $231.00

Charles King: $304.00

Henrietta Smith: $838.28

Walter Smith: $6,686.63

John Sampson: $12,137.53

Walter Sampson: $7,291.55

Onie Snakeya: $5,400.48

Garfield Adams: $1,196.85

Bettie Postoak

Bettie Postoak

Annie Thomas: $9,215.04

Ambrose Thomas

Theo. Roosevelt Thomas: $881.66

Mary Adams: $390.00

Opal Thompson: $231.52

Raymond Thompson

Luncinda Thompson

Amanda Thompson: $1,500.00

Virgie Hooks: $289.91

Annie Wilson: $844.35

Emus Wilson: $846.00

Martin W. Smith: $266.93

Harpley Johnson: $30.00

Haber Johnson: $151.67

Wilson Beaver: $470.95

Sarah Colbert: $1,617.09

Phatimma Smith: $164.13

Steve J. Smith: $108.89

Albert K. Smith: $198.53

Daniel Beaver: $473.86

Sam Marsey

Clarence Jackson

Ben Jackson: $73.50

Laura King: $253.50

Katie Berryhill: $569.79

Peggy Berryhill: $660.25

Benny Stevens

Dewey Stevens

Isparecher Stevens

Davis Berryhill: $461.30

James Thomas, Jr.: $2,766.09

Beatrice Smith: $134.50

Inglish Smith: $134.50

Roy Lee Parker: $175.00

Orvel Dean Dilsaver: $1,682.50

Robert Lowe Dilsaver: $1,660.75

James Colbert

Lillie Colbert: $780.00

Ellis Bird: $1,129.65

Kizzie Bird: $1,139.74

Alice Cuff: $8,357.72

Willie Grayson

Lena Nelson: $232.10

Johnson Roberts: $139.00

Bettie Kanard: $3,854.03

Thomas B. Kanard: $5,046.86

Stella Sands: $801.19

George B. Grissom: $847.00

Viola M. Grissom: $387.64

Fred M. Grissom: $259.60

Nellie Cooper: $1,912.64

Rosa Cooper: $1,892.64

Emma Colbert: $147.80

Minnie Thomas: $40.00

Liza Jans Dill: $414.25

Freddie James Dice: $465.00

Elmer Dice: $44.80

Jackson Monday

McKinley Monday

Christian Grayson: $450.14

Johnston Theo. Lewis: $332.30

Sarah Harjo: $1,845.37

David C. Reynolds: $2,822.68

Jerry J. Reynolds: $2,687.06

Gladys G. Ingley: $185.00

Clarence Hawkins: $294.93

Kellop Hawkins: $208.11

George Hawkins: $40.00

Frank Hawkins: $326.51

Robert Hawkins: $194.69

Pearlie Thompson

Willie Thompson

Bettie Thompson

Frank Thompson

Roman Burge: $224.59

Effie Carr: $594.37

Annie Monday: $197.70

Hillibe Micco Henry: $20.78

Tchinina Henry: $21.93

Amos Watson: $76.50

Freeland Starr: $61.12

Frank Gooden: $493.00

Katie Fixico

Viola Colbert: $283.94

Jesse Davis: $289.91

Ethel Harjo: $309.48

Louisa Stake: $5,921.48

Washie Riley: $233.40

May Summer: $114.00

Pet Summer: $160.00

Joe Hicks: $245.00

Coody Tiger: $414.85

John Haynes: $182.49

Minnie Tiger: $2,203.00

London Marshall: $628.87

Judy Marshall: $655.25

Wiley Sampson: $666.75

Lizie Foster: $538.62

Oyama Wisener: $855.65

Minnie Wisener: $860.25

Bessie Wisener: $890.05

Helen Grayson: $754.50

Hannah Fife: $296.08

Una Fife: $336.10

Josep Fife: $296.10

Florence Rentie: $316.18

Florence Rentie: $200.48

Ora Woodard: $21.50

Otto McCrary: $190.51

Tar-sa-co-con-thal Slaley: $377.00

Theodore Grayson: $15,000.00

India Roberts: $191.50

William Lunsford: 686.86

Charley Lunsford: $910.94

Ida Lunsford: $417.27

Ada Lunsford: $74.38

Susie Lunsford: $74.38

Winnie Lunsford: $5,612.34

Paul Lunsford: $832.34

John Lunsford: $927.86

Ben Lunsford: $637.03

Hattie Lunsford: $466.43

Eliza West: $8.80

Kizzie West: $232.15

George West: $43.10

Russell Thompson: $40.00

Arthur Colbert: $45.00

Willie Manuel: $50.00

John Daniels: $82.30

Annie Daniels

Joseph Burgus

Eliza May Burgus

Willie Harjo

James Adams: $211.25

Castella Thomas: $160.00

Rosa Thomas: $160.00

Jennie Stake: $271.81

Elizabeth Stake: $271.91

Willie Canard: $80.00

Topley Powell: $200.00

Zella Colbert: $350.00

George Colbert: $80.00

Lemuel E. Colbert: $442.00

Eliza Taylor

Eugene Moty Tiger: $2,199.98

CHAPTER 30

Eben approaches the office of Kosom Wade, a mixed-blood Choctaw Attorney. One thing becomes apparent when you view Wade's office and that is its size. The sign outside looks like a billboard in front of an outhouse. Kosom had apparently not moved past his culture and is already twenty-three minutes late according to his posted office hours.

"Is that you, Ebenezer Baker?" Kosom smiles ear to ear, his robust belly straining against suspenders attached to buttons with frayed thread. His tie looked sun-faded, decorated with food stains.

"What you know, *Koni* (Skunk)!" Eben says this, knowing that only someone from Kosom's childhood could get away with mocking him.

"You are a skunk, stinkbutt! I hope you didn't come wanting money, because I don't have any. And, I don't take chickens as payment anymore. Those last Bandy roosters I got apparently didn't know how to get away from a chicken-snake," Kosom says, insinuating that Eben is a freeloader; as a Chahta retort it is par for the course—first attack the honor. "How long has it been? A year maybe? Wait, I know when I saw you last. It was during that singing at Honobia, wasn't it?

Eben nods and smiles.

"Well, come on in, and leave the door open. It's gonna be hot. May have to go home early." Kosom throws some newspapers from a chair next to his desk onto the floor, then motions for Eben to have a seat. Kosom grabs his modern wooden chair, one with fancy wheels on it, the only thing that doesn't look homemade or used. "Well, there ain't a singin' tonight, so I know this must be something else."

"Something else is right. I've got a problem that involves a little girl and a man-eater." Eben stops talking long enough to read Kosom's face.

"What's the matter?"

"Her parents have died. I am getting suspicious now. Anyways, their property went according to a Determination of Heirs with the BIA, and then Judge Skinner appointed Attorney Smith out of Wilburton as her guardian." Eben notices that Kosom covers his mouth. "The Dawes clerk that did the census card was none other than Robert Morgan, the same one that Battiest and I tried to net a long time ago during that Postoak ordeal that involved that Red Oak property."

"Ya'll went too far on that case!" Kosom bristles.

"Nita (Bear) Postoak knew better than to take money from white men! Wait, wait, I don't want to argue anymore with you, Kosom. It's all old and we need to bury the bad blood!"

"He would have made an excellent Micco and you know it! At least he would not have sold out like the Dawes bunch. Battiest controlled the information that got to the Senate, and you know that Jones wanted to take out any Jacob Jackson allies. You guys handed him over to sell-outs." Kosom's face suggests he is determined, though sturggling, to restrain his anger.

"I've said it before, Kosom, if we hadn't investigated the Red River Case the tribe would have gotten even more screwed. You knew as well as I that we were fighting an uphill battle, and we didn't even have Parker in our corner anymore once they moved everything to Muskogee. We were playing the only cards we had left, and if we didn't get Postoak to roll over on his contacts we could not produce enough evidence to charge the Texas Louisiana with fraud. Texas Louisiana was giving everyone against us Indians free rides back east and there is no telling how many they paid off. You know as well as I that they had judges and congressmen in their pockets. Postoak should have known who he was dealing with! Wait Wait! I'm not here about that. I'm here about Annie Meshaya!

Kosom turns his head to look out his front window. Choctaws usually express dissent by moving away, and Kosom found the vacant stare his only option.

"Kosom, I'm sorry that we went after your friend so hard, I thought we were doing the right thing. After we thought the election was stolen in the Moshulatubbee District we became alarmed that the Progressives were going to start dismantling the department since the National won the Treasury and Secretary seats. Battiest was concerned that they had enough votes to try to say we were in collusion with Postoak. We were very afraid they would defund the department and then all our schools would have shut down during the fight. It would have been out of the frying pan into the fire for our legal fight with Red River Company, and those white men would have gotten off; you remember how members of the Progressives wanted to sign the agreement and sell all our minerals. We were convinced that some of the Progressives were in bed with the Red River Company. No white man would get any of our school money as long as Battiest was in the Treasury."

Kosom turns to give Eben, not a look of contempt or pity, but one of interest. "Why did you go after Nita? He hit his term limits and would no longer be Auditor. If he got the election he could have challenged the Atoka Agreement and you know it!"

"Kosom, I went in and began investigating, hoping to find something on some of the Progressives and discredit them. Jones and his family heard that we were checking them out and I dug fast so that they couldn't cover their tracks. Looking back, I was doing the investigation for the wrong reason. I chose a path that was not trying to redeem anyone. All I could see was those who came to steal and those who were helping them. When I found the letters from Red River to N. Postoak I felt betrayed and consumed with vengeance. I know that vengeance is the Lord's, but I still wanted someone to be prosecuted for the way things were, the way we were losing everything again, like in Mississippi. I honestly thought Nita knew more and would confess to knowing who Morgan was, or at least name one of the other players in the Pine-Oak Company or the Red River one. Now one of the players is a Judge over a little girl who has lost so much."

Eben looks at the floor, ashamed that he had played the political game well—too well. He had discovered long ago that the amount of energy you use to persecute will be the amount that will persecute you, even if you are fighting the good fight but do so with the wrong motive. Lucifer loves a deceived David. And then. . .

"Well, you're right, it is old blood. Who'd have figured that we would end up on the same side? Both as useless as boar's tits." Kosom still gazes outside, but now not so distantly, and his voice is not from that deep defensive tone but the compassionate one hidden in the strongest warriors. "This girl is Annie you say? And we can't file in Wilburton because the Judge is the one who appointed Smith right?"

"If we file there we will not get so much as a breath of a chance. While I was in Muskogee, I was told by a former Cherokee Representative I knew from the old days that the Supreme Court in Oklahoma City is filled with former Railroad Attorneys. If we try to get her case heard on grounds of protection granted under a treaty you know how those former Boomers will interpret the law on appeal. With the BIA coming in as a friend of the court on the Guardianship it will look like we are the only ones challenging her guardianship, and Smith already made it sound like I was just after Annie's money."

Eben closes his eyes and looks like he scanning for answers behind the lids, as if God is going to program some type of answer in a vision.

"Ebenezer, that's not the worst of it." Kosom looks under piles of paper and then recovers a newspaper from under one stack. On the front page is an article about the formation of a "Committee on Indian Depredations." There, in the second paragraph, is a name everyone in Indian Territory knows: the former Indian Agent of the Muskogee Agency. This same man is elected by the State Legislature as the first Senator from the new State of Oklahoma. His oil wealth in Tulsa rivals Frank Phillips and Senator Todd Blue, wealth that, with his generous donations, will have buildings in Bartlesville named for him. Senator Owen claimed he was Cherokee and then stole Cherokee lands. Appointing him to the committee will be like appointing Mengele to investigate atrocities committed at Dachau.

CHAPTER 31

The headline of the *New York Times,* on March 3, 1915, proclaims "KATE BARNARD ASKS HELP: Wants 13 Bills Killed to Prevent Robbing of Indians. Miss Kate Barnard, State Commissioner of Charities of Oklahoma, who charges that there is a systematic plot to rob Indian full-bloods and minor heirs of Oklahoma of more than $200,000,000 worth of coal lands, has just issued a last appeal calling for the defeat of thirteen bills in the House and Senate which she alleges will work great harm to the Indians. She claims 'If Oklahoma grafters have their way, this money and land will be distributed now.'"

Kate may have been the only white person who, upon discovery of the evidence, would have asked "Was Ullie murdered?" A pertinent question about an eight-year-old who was found hanged. Perhaps it was suicide. But then her cousin was hanged as well. The irony would have filled Kate with rage. Eighteen thousand investigations, or one an hour, would take 750 days without sleep. One woman against a plethora of state lawyers, elected men who will soon make Oklahoma one of the few states where the legislature is controlled by a majority who are proud to be members of the Ku Klux Klan.

Kate is rumored to have said, "I have been compelled to see orphans robbed, starved, and burned for money. I have named the men and accused them and furnished the records and affidavits to convict them, but with no result. I decided long ago that Oklahoma had no citizen who cared whether or not an orphan is robbed or starved or killed - because his dead claim is easier to handle than if he were alive."

Kate will move into the obscure corners of history to be forgotten. But the names of the orphans still call from her.

In 1911, $3,000 could buy a house worth $177,600 today. Perhaps Kate knew in the end that, for native children who had no parents, there never was a place like home. Silver slippers or ruby, some dreams only belong to people who sing "where the wind comes sweepin down the plain."

Payne County would have originally been under the protection of the Cherokee Nation's Cherokee Outlet District. It became portions of the Pawnee, Otoe Missouria, and Sac & Fox reservations. Ironically, township 19, in Payne County, is adjacent to the Muscogee Nation Cushing Oil Field and is named Eagle. Pawnee families with the surname Eagle had allotments in that township next to the Muscogee Nation. David Eagle died before the allotment. Was Toochie married to a half Pawnee? When the smallpox outbreak happened near the Sac & Fox, were David and Toochie early victims, thus leaving Ullie to become an orphan? The Pawnee Reservation was adjacent to the Sac & Fox. Eagle is also a name among many Cherokee allottees. At any rate, Winney Tiger's census card does name Haton Harjo as her father, and the court recorder named David's dad as Hathan. Did Hathan/Haton have a preexisting relationship with a Cherokee lady or a Pawnee lady? Toochie was the aunt of Ullie through her father, Santale Fixico.

Pittsburg County would have originally been under the protection of the Choctaw Nation's Moshulatubbee District in Tobucksy and segments of Gaines County. It would have become Tobuxsy and Hailey counties in the Indian state of Sequoyah.

Pontotoc County would have originally been under the protection of the Chickasaw Nation's Pontotoc County. It would have become Cheadle and Mosely counties in the Indian state of Sequoyah.

Pushmataha County would have originally been under the protection of the Choctaw Nation's Pushmataha District in Cedar, Jacks Fork, and segments of Kiamichi and Wade counties. It would have become Pushmataha and portions of Hitchcock and Blue counties in the Indian state of Sequoyah.

PAYNE COUNTY

Russell F. Kelley

Eddie T. Kelley: $1,604.50

Samuel L. Moor

Sadora Neal: $366.35

Daniel S. Hunter

Maude Kakague: $1,215.78

Lee Bars: $252.58

lone C. Bars: 286.98

Ben Hull: $365.84

PITTSBURG COUNTY

Willie Carrol

Sampson Cole

Joe Ott

Simeon Ott

Annie En-shawk-ey

Lynch Arpealer

Insbia Stibling

Edna Stibling

Edna Stibling

Marv A. Stibling

Joe Morris

PONTOTOC COUNTY

Mami Porter

Dillard Perry

Gertrude Bruner: $400.00

Dillard Perry: $1,250.00

Joe Perry: $1,250.00

Lilly Grain

Testa Grain

Eunice Grain

Flossa Grain: $1,861.82

Berwin Grain

Oscar Grain

Ella Perry

Charley Perry

Nellie Robinson

Winnie Robinson

Aris Robinson: $273.50

Carrol M. Spann

Claude E. Spann: $1,708.84

Gaston Hickman: $1,440.00

Enid Holloway: $500.00

Ida L. Budes

Mattie Helen Lewis

Mabel Lawrence

Tillie Lawrence

Mattie Lawrence

George Lawrence: $376.25

Eller Summers

John McNeil

Bill McNeil

Sallie McNeil

Cubby Colbert

Martha L. Spann: $2,000.00

Franklin Porter

Viola Clark

Fleet Clark: $480.00

Effie Goft

E. F. Goft

May Paul

PUSHMATAHA COUNTY

Johnson Felihkatabbee: $5,000.00

Caroline Cole

John Peter

ROGER MILLS COUNTY (Cheyenee & Arapaho)

Lola A. Rhodes: $154.00

John Hensley

Joseph Hensley

Joseph Stites: $1,600.00

CHAPTER 32

Eben leaves Kosom Wade's office depressed. He heads north out of town over the mountain road between Talihina and Leflore, a community en route to Red Oak. It is late and he decides to go again to Rock Creek for shelter.

"Hello, sprinkler." Pastor Meshaya teases him about not being Baptist as he walks from the parsonage to take the harness of Eben's horse.

"How are you, drowner?"

"Well, how is that little girl you came by here last time about?

Eben lies, "She's just fine."

"You find out what you needed to know about her money?

"Not yet. Still trying to understand how anyone would treat her so badly."

"You know I was meaning to tell you last time you were here and so now I will. The Scripture says that the love of money is idolatry. When you deal with idolaters you are dealing with people who have a different God than we do. Now to us the way they treat people doesn't make any sense, that's because we believe the first will be the last. They think that all that money will somehow make them greater, not knowing that God humbles the proud. I don't care who you are, if you steal you will be haunted by the ghosts of your bad doing."

Eben is steps down from the wagon and he reaches out to shake Pastor Meshaya's hand. "It's good to see you, Pastor."

"It's good to be seen on any day other than Sunday. Sometimes all I see is the backside of Squirrel and Chipmunk." He says this, pointing at his farm mules chewing hay in the pasture. The mules look at the men with curiosity.

"You able to get much planted?"

"Oh, I got them to till, but I can't convince 'em to go pick that corn for me. I figure I'll get my wife Hattie too," Pastor Meshaya giggles.

"Exia would tell me to go chase my tail."

"Oh, Hattie will tell me the same, so I won't ask her to until after supper."

Eben manages to turn in early that night after supper and some conversation. He doesn't sleep well at all. The heat makes his face radiate anxiety. That morning, he puts on his shirt and shoes, steps outside and harnesses his horse to the wagon, and leaves without saying goodbye. He leaves two dollars and a thank-you note on his pillow. He pushes a letter to his wife into his jacket and shakes the reins to start the horse walking. The horse walks steadily north to Red Oak and then he turns the wagon west towards Wilburton.

He rides into Wilburton driving the wagon beneath a shade tree, watching the front of the court house. He watches people come and go and then spots a familiar, hated face: Skinner's. Judge Skinner is preparing to take lunch at home or at a lunch room and he strolls from the building towards a Ford Model T. The car is the first ever bought and driven in Wilburton, a demarcation of his opulence. He calls to a deputy who walks over and cranks the motor to life. Skinner releases the brake handle to put the car in gear. Under the canopy of shade Eben retrieves his thirty-ought-six from under his seat. He slides a round into the chamber and cocks the lever. It is simple, all he has to do is put the sight between the notches and let justice fly. He knows what the kick will feel like, the sudden shove against his shoulder and the roar as the bullet flies. He knows that others will fly back at him from stunned officers running about the court building like red wasps do when you pick up a wood shingle to expose their nest. What he doesn't know is how he will feel after Skinner bleeds out. Will he feel righteous or slimy? He can see it in his mind. Suddenly he feels God's disapproval in the face of Exia, her sad, disconsolate expression framing his sin.

"Father, why won't you just cause him to fall dead like Sapphira? Why do you tolerate such evil? He will not stop until Annie is dead, Lord! You know this! Please, I need a sign that what I am doing is the right thing. I know that you said 'Bless those who curse us,' but he isn't cursing me but rather an innocent little girl. Am I not saving her from the clutches of Molech? Why do you let this happen?"

No sign, no lightning, no thunder, no wind, no silent voice. Eben feels his leg leaving the wagon his chest constricted and tight. The rifle heavy and his fingers strain to maintain the anger. Suddenly Skinner's Model T stops running. Skinner's balding head leans out and then he steps out of it to check something. Eben will not follow Skinner to shoot him in secret, nor will he run—it would be dishonorable; if he is going to kill him it has to be in front of a hall of justice. The more Eben stands in silence, the more he feels the hatred bleed away. He spent all night visualizing how he would drop this man. He has spent months thinking of him as the epitome of a Baal worshipper, sacrificing children to the idolatrous god of greed. Suddenly, everything is clear: hate will never surrender its gravity! Love, like light, must fight like hell to maintain its orbit. Eben loosens his grip and puts the rifle on the floor of his wagon. He steps into the wagon, jostles the reins, and turns away to leave hate. Sometimes the hearts of Lions do not fear their prey, sometimes they fear what will happen to the cubs should they fall.

Somewhere that night, Kialegee, Tvkabatche, Alabama and many others dance around a fire, hoping that a new day, a new year, will bring healing and love. Somewhere a fire burns in the dark and light craves a renewal of humanity. Somewhere people look towards the dawn.

CHAPTER 33

Letter from Kate Barnard

The first page of this letter from RG 36–1 Box 46 Folder 26 in the Oklahoma Department of Libraries, Oklahoma State Archives, containing Kate Barnard Records, is not in the folder.

> Page 2
> OKLAHOMA DISGRACED
>
> Within a year after the Oklahoma delegation had compelled Congress to remove its jurisdiction over the Indian estates, and place this jurisdiction in the county courts of Oklahoma, a wholesale robbery of Indians, even including Indian orphan children, came about that Everybody's Magazine contained a long article entitled: "Oklahoma's Shame." This brought to my attention this condition in Indian affairs, but even without this article I should shortly have known of the robbery as it had become as wide-spread as to be a matter of statewide and even national comment.
>
> DEPARTMENT OF CHARITIES ENTERS FIGHT.
>
> DEPARTMENT OF CHARITIES WRECKED.
>
> At this state of the game I went before the Third Legislature of Oklahoma and secured, after a most bitter battle, an appropriation for one attorney to protect the orphan children of these tribes. I prosecuted without fear or favor, and the result was that the Fourth Legislature wrecked the Department of Charities after they had made a vain effort to compel me to appoint an attorney,

Frank Montgomery, who the leaders in the House of Representatives demanded should be placed in charge of the prosecution of Indian affairs in the Department of Charities.

EASTERN PHILATHROPISTS ENTER FIGHT.

At this state of the fight Eastern organizations composed of philanthropists, sociologists, political economists, scientists, and statesmen furnished money to the Department of Charities in Oklahoma to carry on its fight for the Indians. The Mohonk Conference for Indians took a hand in the fight. Its members contributed liberally and the body passed the following resolution at its October meeting of 1914:

"Conditions in the State of Oklahoma, affecting particularly the Five Civilized Tribes, call for the closest scrutiny. In the Event that the Oklahoma legislature shall fail to give early and adequate protection to these Indians, we see no alternative but that the Federal Government should resume full jurisdiction over all of the 'Restricted' Indians of that State."

The men who furnished me with the means of fighting for these Indians, some of them belong to the most substantial families in America, who have been interested in the protection of Indians since the time of William Penn. These men who have made the protection of Indians a life study have mapped out a program for me to follow here in Oklahoma, a program which we believe is the only possible method which will assure protection to the helpless Indians of this state. They ask that I go before the Oklahoma Legislature and secure an appropriation for the necessary attorneys in the Department of Charities to properly protect the Indian orphans of the State.

Secondly. They demand that the rules of probate procedure promulgated by the Supreme Court which became effective July 25, 1914, be legalized by legislative law. Following their instructions I introduced Senate Bill #350, through Senator Russell and McIntosh a copy of which I herewith enclose; a bill which simply provides that our Department shall have two attorneys whose duty it shall be to inquire into the need and necessity of the sale or mortgage of Indian orphan lands and that no such sale or mortgage can be made until after such inquiry.

DETERMINED TO ROB INDIAN ORPHANS.

I went before the committee and made a desperate appeal for the favorable report on this bill, but the committee voted to kill the bill. Finally I prevailed on the committee to allow the bill to come out without a report and be placed on the calendar, since which time I have been unable even to secure a discussion on the same.

SUPREME COURT RULES HAVE NOT STANDING IN COURT.

The Decision on the Tiger case which was recently handed down shows that the rules of procedure promulgated by the supreme-court are not compulsory. The result is that the federal probate attorneys appointed by the Government to protect these Indians have no jurisdiction, no power and no authority. The county judge may kindly permit them to practice in his court, but in the last campaign county judges were running on the express platform that if elected "they would not allow federal attorneys to appear in their courts."

INDIAN ORPHANS WITHOUT PROTECTION.

Thus the Federal attorneys have no power or authority to protect these Indians and the Department of Charities, which is empowered by special enactment of the legislature, has no appropriation. More than that, the fifth legislature refuses to give you more than your own salary and a stenographer. Should you force them to give you one attorney—one attorney could not do more than one-half this work. In fact, my bill as I drew it provided for five attorneys and it was only after a long drawn-out wrangle that I consented to allow Senate bill 350 to be introduced providing for only two attorneys. I should not have made this concession but for the fact that you thought you could get through an appropriation for an assistant who would be an attorney and thus I felt the three layers would be able to cover most of this territory and to protect the fifteen or twenty thousand Indian orphan children, whose destinies are at stake.

WHOLESALE ROBBERY OF INDIAN ORPHANS CONTEMPLATED.

Ever since this legislature convened I have had two men and two women and one detective working on the same, examining every bill. Sounding out the sentiment of the body and getting information which will later prove fairly interesting to the people of this nation. I enclose herewith copy of a part of this information which I sent out to thousands of voters of the state by yesterday's mail.

LEGISLATURE PROMOTES THIS INDIAN GRAFT.

You will notice that I have listed therein thirteen bills introduced in the present legislature. Every one of which will promote the graft and robbery of Indian orphan children. This was why I called you over the telephone this morning and suggested to you that it might be possible for you to secure aid for your Department from Washington. I have a communication which states that it might be possible to secure from Congress, an appropriation for attorneys in your Department. I told you this over the telephone and your answer was that you were a thorough believer in states' rights and that you did not want to receive Federal appropriations, and because I am your friend and wish to be perfectly fair, I have made this survey of the fight, giving you a history of same in order that you might have the facts before you in this matter.

If you still feel after reading the letter, that you do not want to accept a Federal appropriation because you, as a Democrat are still standing by the theory of states' rights, I wish you would simply drop me a line, stating this, in order that it may place me right before the public. Because of course, I presume you would follow out my own policies and I therefore agreed to the demands of the Mohonk Conference and the others who are furnishing the funds for this fight when they suggested that the most feasible plan for the protection of the Indians of Oklahoma would be, first, to place the Department of Charities in a position to fight, and secondly, to legalize the standing of the Federal attorneys so that through these attorneys the government could make its fight. As you know, I have fought hard through the whole legislature to assist you in securing appropriations for your own department and I have stood by you as one friend stands by another and my only purpose in writing this letter is because I am compelled to do so in order that I may not proceed with a policy which would be distasteful to you.

Please drop me a simple line stating whether or not you would accept a federal appropriation or whether you would be disbarred by doing so by your loyalty to the democratic principle of states' rights.

In making your decision, consider whether the states' rights theory would hold your conscience after the state has refused to act to prevent a great human wrong.

Yours sincerely,
Signed Kate Barnard
P. S.

> Of course it would be ridiculous to get this appropriation for you unless you were in such thorough accord that you would enter the fight with the spirit and the determination to protect these orphans. I should not want to be responsible for securing the appropriation unless you felt thoroughly in accord with the proposition after reading the material herewith enclosed.
>
> I am sure you will do me the courtesy, which I would do you, namely; to make an immediate reply.
>
> KB/M.

Seminole County would have originally been under the protection of the Seminole Nation. It would have remained Seminole County in the Indian state of Sequoyah.

Sequoyah County would have originally been under the protection of the Cherokee Nation's Illinois, Canadian, and Sequoyah districts. It would have become Sequoyah and Breckinridge counties in the Indian state of Sequoyah.

Tulsa County would have originally been under the protection of the Muscogee Nation's Coweta and Okmulgee districts. It would have become Euchee County in the Indian state of Sequoyah.

SEMINOLE COUNTY

Lena Wolf: $812.40

George Joseph

Anday Joseph: $700.00

Gemima Joseph: $205.40

Willie Joseph: $213.94

Lowiney Joseph: $392.14

Thomas Grayson: $564.00

Stella Warris: $1,200.00

Henderson Samuels

Sampson Samuels

Lula Samuels

Timmie Wolf

SEQUOYAH COUNTY

Mamie Leigh: $65.85

Langford Leigh: $600.03

Floyd Leigh: $509.65

Arthur Leigh: $521.68

Georgia Couch: $201.22

Sadie Carrell: $73.00

Phillip W. Carrell: $250.00

May Thomas: $769.08

Bonnie Thomas: $771.98

Addie Lee: $800.00

Charles Denny

Emma Denny: $83.32

Prince Crim

Prudie Crim

Chauncy Crim

John Lee Kennedy: $133.19

William Riley Kennedy: $133.19

Clarence N. Pitts

Ben Wildcat

William J. Largins: $279.59

John To Largins: $226.52

Taylor Cotton

Wisdom Jesse Cotton

Elizabeth Cotton

Kilrain Cotton: $9,700.00

Irene May Capps

Warlena Springwater

Lujean Adair

James C. Adair: $2,329.44

Thomas Adair

Addie Lee: $412.50

Phillip W. Carrell: $500.00

Jim Tehee: $582.40

Phillip W. Carrell: $250.00

Jim Tehee: $640.00

Belle Altus

STEPHENS COUNTY

Thelma Lee Spain: $168.35

Leldia Perry

Rine Perry: $3,000.00

J. T. Clark, et al: $167.16

Lucy T. Clark: $55.72

Minnie May Spain: $119.00

TULSA COUNTY

Hennie Wiley

Lena Mathews: $532.21

Thomas Blair

Leroy Roach: $1,040.00

Jerome Flippin

Hugh Elmer Bud: $696.66

Hugh Elmer Bird: $1,696.38

Annie Davis

Victoria Davis

Mattie Burgeus: $1,174.38

Flossie M. England: $1,974.70

Louie B. England: $1,459.36

Elva May Garnes: $4,100.00

Henry Evans: $35.00

Mattie Evans: $183.21

Albert Lee Evans: $1,407.06

Esther Runyan: $980.68

Samuel Runyan: $993.32

Holland H. Boles: $4,560.00

Beatrice Tiblon: $1,476.44

Samuel Charley: $5,427.59

Ruth Ketcher: $715.00

Minnie Ketcher: $715.00

Harvey Ketcher: $174.00

Robert Mcintosh

Morris Sheppard

Etha Sheppard

Edna Sheppard: $2,604.80

Viola Johnson: $188.09

David Johnson: $265.70

Georgie Mayfield: $160.00

Joseph Perryman: $450.00

Lee A. Posey: $1,355.86

Wm. A. Posey: $13,000.00

Mary E. Posey

Melisa Harkey

Bessie Fife: $1,536.19

Bessie Fife: $1,536.19

Linda Tyner: $1,788.38

George H. Tucker

William Tucker

Floyd C. Tucker: $4,380.00

William C. Charley: $54.00

John Douglas Thatcher

Edna Franklin Thatcher

Charles De Thatcher $557.71

Sarah A. Perryman: $2,000.00

Sarah A. Perryman: $450.00

Clarence Crow: $513.92

Wm. Crow: $100.00

Gertrude Grayson

Ella Grayson

Ethel Alton

Perryman Buck: $2,500.00

Rosella Kelly

Kissie Kelley: $350.78

Norah Parnoski: $3,300.63

Bettie McHenry: $160.00

Abbie McHenry: $160.00

Oliver Lee Withers: $320.00

Joseph A. Withers: $208.00

Cully Barnett

Lillie Barnett: $1,781.68

Matthew Dyer: $400.00

Mary Frailey, nee Ishmael

Virgia Childers: $22,063.03

Richard Childers: $260.00

Virgia Childers: $23.396.73

Earle E. Drew

Jimmie Ray Drew: $800.00

Cherokee Izola Minton

Jesse McHenry

Dave McHenry: $3,100.00

Nat Adkins

Charles Tiblow: $3,465.86

Bertha Tiblow: $1,651.07

Geo. H. Tucker.

William Tucker

WASHINGTON COUNTY

Josephine Rider

WASHITA COUNTY

Erma Henry

Ellen Henry

Edice Asel Henry

Asel Eddie Henry

Thomas W. Henry

Floyd Henry

Samuel Henry

John Henry

Andrew Peterson

Irene Peterson

Helena Klassen: $564.00

Robert Warden

Weter heirs: $188.61

Otis Burrow: $880.45

Lewis C. Ledbetter

Thomas Ledbetter: $415.72

WOODS COUNTY

Beulah Hamilton

Earl Hamilton

Robert Lee Litton: $151.80

WOODWARD COUNTY

Clarence Endicott

Joseph Endicott

Clella Endicott

Beula Endicott: $5,763.50

CHAPTER 34

TO PROMOTE THE GENERAL WELFARE OF THE INDIANS OF OKLAHOMA
MONDAY, APRIL 22, 1935
House of Representatives,
Committee on Indian Affairs,
Washington, DC.

The committee this day met at 10:30 a.m., Hon. Will Rogers, chairman, presiding, for consideration of H.R. 6234, which reads as follows:

{H.R. 6234, 74th Cong., 1st sess.}

A BILL to propose the general welfare of the Indians of the State of Oklahoma—

The Chairman: You say that the most egregious cases of child deprivation occurred around that time?

Mr. Collier: Yes, that period around statehood saw exploitation on a scale that is, excuse me Chairman, I would like to cite the case of Ledcie Stechie if I may?

The Chairman: Continue.

Mr. Collier: Ledcie Stechie, a Choctaw minor, was allotted property with coal. Her estate was worth nearly two hundred and sixty thousand dollars ($260,000) at the time of her tragic death. In 1924, Zitkala-Sa joined Charles Fabens and Matthew Sniffen to write a report entitled "Oklahoma's Poor Rich Indians—An Orgy of Graft and Exploitation of the Five Civilized Tribes-Legalized Robbery." They uncovered that her court-appointed guardian attempted to take her from her grandmother. The grandmother had Ledcie placed at Wheelock Academy. There Ledcie did well in school and she had generous provision of food and shelter. Her guardian with legal documents seized her from the academy. She was found dead, having died from malnutrition, Chairman. . .The guardian inherited her estate under the dead Indian provisions outlined by Congress.

FINAL THOUGHT

When the Seminole Oil Field went through, one oil man, Jake Hamon, had become impatient about expanding his empire further. Hamon literally paid $1,000,000 to the campaign of Republican Warren Harding to secure the Secretary of Interior slot for himself. Hamon wanted to open Wyoming's Tea-Pot dome for drilling. Hamon's mistress found out that she was not invited to DC. Apparently Hamon was scared of scandal. She shot him. Not even a happy ending; she was no masseuse.

Harry Sinclair, yes the dinosaur on signs by Sinclair Oil, with his bank in Tulsa, saw an opportunity. He gave over a quarter million to the new Secretary of Interior Falls. Ultimately, Sinclair and Secretary Fall would be sentenced to prison at club fed. Oklahoma's corruption because of the oil industry is legendary. It's not in Oklahoma history textbooks though. Prevenient grace appearing in sins of omission.

When the Oklahoma Indian Welfare Act was introduced, Tulsa's and Oil's representative to Congress, Representative Disney, would claim that reestablishing tribal governments was to invite socialistic enclaves into the state; if calling someone a "communist" sounds familiar, then you have seen Ku Klux Klan propaganda. Throw in some Catholic hate and you have a good ol' Okie fish fry. If Oklahoma means "Red People" in Choctaw, then the name would be apropos if you think like the Oil Industry's man. Disney was sitting in a committee and painting Red Men red during a Red Scare. Tribal people had gone from merciless savages to become bourgeois or more appropriately under Rep. Disney's ilk, proletariat.

Frank Baum, the author of *Oz*, called for the extermination of the Indian. Maybe the better angels like Kate, or maybe the Good Witch Glinda, prevailed? Maybe "Somewhere Over the Rainbow" cannot be translated into Choctaw or Muscogee as easily as Oklahoma and Estecate. Maybe a pot of gold is a pot of oil just over the rainbow.

AFTERWORD

I had spent years tracking down any information on Ullie Eagle. Since I had been working on my doctorate the research was hit-or-miss. It all started in the 1990s, when I worked for the Kialegee Tribal Town. I came across the congressional testimony of Muscogee Mekko Roly Canard before Congress. I then read the reports on the death of tribal minors with substantial mineral wealth. That is when I read about Ledcie Stechie. She was found dead in the community of Smithville.

Later when I was conducting research on my great-grandfather, Ben Carterby, I discovered that prior to WWI he had been an Indian Police Officer for the Bureau of Indian Affairs. His jurisdiction was around the communities of Bethel, Battiest, and Smithville. I haven't stopped wondering if he had been an investigator of Ledcie's death? Did he discover the guardian appointed by the county judge? Then I wondered if Ben's evidence was part of the documentation during the hearings for the Oklahoma Indian Welfare Act, part of the evidence I read. Because Ben Carterby had been educated at Jones Academy, he could speak, read, and write in English as well as Choctaw. Thus he was one of the fourteen Choctaw Codetalkers awarded medals posthumously for his service in WWI. The state of Oklahoma recently honored him with the naming of a bridge. The sign is outside of Smithville.

When I was at Kialegee Tribal Town conducting my research I came across the name of the little girl Ullie Eagle. I found out she had been hanged. During my research I then found the transcripts of her case at the Oklahoma Historical Society. There was a name I recognized but did not associate with anything. The name was Nellie Fish. When I got Nellie's allotment record, there it was in clear sight. She was Kialegee, thus her mother was Kialegee, but her father was Artusse. I knew some descendants of the Fish family intimately. In fact, when my mother died, a Kialegee woman of the Raccoon Clan, Sylvanna Caldwell, started calling me her Choctaw Son. I call her Wotko (Raccoon) Mom. Sylvanna had been on the Muscogee National Council representing the Tvkvbatche District back in the early 2000s. Sylvanna and I have had so many conversations about the Muscogee people's ways and our mutual friend Melissa Harjo have filled in so many nuances of culture that I am beyond blessed. Sylvanna mentioned her parents dying when she was a girl and thus she was sent to boarding school at Chilocco. She also mentioned coming home to Wetumka and seeing her grandmother. She mentioned that her grandmother was Nellie Fish. I don't know why I didn't put it together. She is the daughter of Kialegee and grandchild of Artusse. When I see her face I now can guess what Ullie's smile would have looked like had she grown to be seventy. I gave Sylvanna one of the first draft copies of this book.

I raised my three daughters around Henryetta, Oklahoma. I actually moved there because I had my first job after graduate school as the Director and only staff member of the Department of Indian Child Welfare with the Alabama Quassarte Tribal Town. A side story: I grew up attending church camp at Ringold, Oklahoma with friends that were Alabama Coushatta. Nearby Ringold is the historic community of Alikchi, which means "doctor" in Choctaw. Alikchi is where Maggie Wade is listed during the allotment. Maggie would marry Ben Carterby and their daughter Rhoda is my great-grandmother. At church camp I had many friends, and one was a friend we called "Chipmunk," who was Alabama Coushatta. When I interviewed with the Alabama Quassarte, I asked how the tribes were related and told them of my childhood friends. Henryetta is also the home of the Indian Home Guard warrior Chitto Harjo. Chitto Harjo followed Opothleyahola in evacuating a large number of Upper Creeks to the Union lines in Kansas. When the Dawes Allotment started, Chitto Harjo became a staunch treaty advocate, demanding his people's land to be sacred under promise of treaty. They called his movement the Snake Movement. When the National Guard was sent in to put down his followers near Hickory Ground, outside of Henryetta, Chitto Harjo was wounded. He evacuated again, with his wounds, to his Choctaw friend Daniel Bobb of Smithville.

Ben Carterby is buried in the Nashoba Indian Cemetery where I have placed a flag every year since my mom passed. Nashoba means "wolf" in Choctaw. I have learned so much among the Muscogee and especially the Kialegee. Mekko Jim Wesley, Betty Hotulke, Sylvanna (Fish) Caldwell, and Melissa Harjo shared so much with me. A Muscogee story tells of how the animals in the first council lead by the bear chose the raccoon's tail to represent life; dark and light, dark and light. You can learn so much from raccoons, wind, fish, bears, and wolves. The Muscogee move around the ceremonial fire in the counterclockwise motion, orbiting the fire they sing. Long before Copernicus they knew life moves in orbit around a fire. The Muscogee and Choctaw move like the bodies of our small solar system and they chant and move and hope and sing.

Life is full of wonder and mystery. I raised my girls near the home of Chitto Harjo, and it feels like the native girls spoke to me across time, as if Ledcie and Ullie were asking me to remember them. I wish I could have been the daddy of Ledcie and Ullie. They would have grown to be beautiful Indian women like I have known all my life.

BIBLIOGRAPHY

"An Act to Provide for the Allotment of Lands in Severalty to Indians on the Various Reservations (General Allotment Act or Dawes Act)." 24 Statutes at Large § NADP document a1887 (1887)

"Annual Report of the Commissioner of Indian Affairs (1881)." http://digital.library.wisc.edu/1711.dl/History.AnnRep81.

"Annual Report of the Commissioner of Indian Affairs (1882)." http://digicoll.library.wisc.edu/cgi-bin/History/History-idx?type=turn&entity=History.AnnRep82.p0018&id=History.AnnRep82&isize=M.

"Annual Report of the Commissioner of Indian Affairs (1895)." http://Digicoll.Library.Wisc.Edu/Cgi-Bin/History/History-Idx?Type=Turn&Entity=History.AnnRep82.P0018&Id=History.AnnRep82&Isize=M.

"Annual Report of the Commissioner of Indian Affairs (1900)." http://digicoll.library.wisc.edu/cgi-bin/History/History-idx?type=goto&id=History.AnnRep1900p2&isize=M&submit=Go+to+page&page=139.

"Annual Report of the Commissioner of Indian Affairs (1902)." https://Digicoll.Library.Wisc.Edu/Cgi-Bin/History/History-Idx?Type=Goto&Id=History.AnnRep02p1&Isize=M&Submit=Go+to+Page&Page=709.

"Annual Report of the Commissioner of Indian Affairs (1904)." https://Digicoll.Library.Wisc.Edu/Cgi-Bin/History/History-Idx?Type=Article&Did=History.AnnRep04p1.I0028&Id=History.AnnRep04p1&Isize=M.

Barnard, Kate. "Fourth Report of the Commissioner of Charities and Corrections." https://babel.hathitrust.org/cgi/pt?id=uc1.b2996269;view=1up;seq=7.

———. *Determined to Rob Indian Orphans.* (1914). (46, Vols. RG 36–1, p. Folder 26). Oklahoma City, Oklahoma.

———. "Kate Barnard Asks Help: Wants 13 Bills Killed to Prevent Robbing of Indians. *New York Times,* March 3, 1915. https://www.nytimes.com/1915/03/03/archives/kate-barnard-asks-help-wants-13-bills-killed-to-prevent-robbing-of.html?searchResultPosition=1.

Benson, H. C. *Life among the Choctaw Indians and Sketches of the South-west.* Cincinnati, OH: L. Swormstedt & A. Poe, 1860.

A Bill for the Better Protection of the Indian Tribes, and Their Consolidation under a Civil Government, to Be Called the Territory of Oklahoma. (S. 653). [U.S. senate]. (1872). http://memory.loc.gov/cgi-bin/ampage?collId=llsb&fileName=042/llsb042.db&recNum=2187.

Bonnin, Gertrude, et al. *Oklahoma's Poor Rich Indians: An Orgy of Graft and Exploitation of the Five Civilized Tribes—Legalized Robbery.* Philadelphia: Office of the Indian Right Association, 1924. https://digitalprairie.ok.gov/digital/collection/culture/id/6553/.

Brown, C. E. *Choctaw Social and Ceremonial Life.* Oklahoma City: Oklahoma Choctaw Council, 1983.

Burton, Jeffrey. *Indian Territory and the United States, 1866–1906.* Norman: University of Oklahoma Press, 1995.

Cain, Del. *Lawmen of the Old West: The Good Guys.* Plano: Republic of Texas Press, 2000.

Casey, Orben J. *And Justice for All: The Legal Profession in Oklahoma, 1821–1989.* Oklahoma City: Western Heritage, 1989.

Chahta Anumpa Aiikhvna. "Trail of Tears from Mississippi Walked by Our Ancestors." www.choctawschool.com/home-side-menu/history/trail-of-tears-from-mississippi-walked-by-our-ancestors.aspx.

Cushman, H. B. *History of the Choctaw, Chickasaw and Natchez Indians.* Greenville, Texas: Headlight, 1899.

Debo, Angie. *The Rise and Fall of the Choctaw Republic.* Norman: University of Oklahoma Press, 1934.

———. *And Still the Waters Run: The Betrayal of the Five Civilized Tribes.* Princenton, NJ: Princeton University Press, 1940.

Deed of Nellie Fish, No. 12806, 1914 (County of Creek September 18, 1914).

Editor. "The Great Seal of the State of Oklahoma (250)." Chronicles of Oklahoma, 1943.

Fish v. kennamer, 37 F.2nd 243 (10th Circuit, U.S. Court of Appeals 1929).

Fuel Oil Journal. (1916, January 1). https://catalog.hathitrust.org/Record/008616593.

Fugate, Tally D. "Anti-Suffrage Association." https://www.okhistory.org/publications/enc/entry.php?entry=AN014.

Hagan, William Thomas. *Indian Police and Judges.* Lincoln: University of Nebraska Press, 1966.

Harmon, Alexandra. (2003). "American Indians and Land Monopolies in the Gilded Age." *The Journal of American History* 90.1 (June 2003) 106–33. http://www.jstor.com/stable/3659793.

Harrington, Fred Harvey. *Hanging Judge.* Norman: University of Oklahoma Press, 1951.

"Harry Sinclair." *The Oil Weekly* (May 28, 1921). https://www.google.com/books/edition/Congressional_Record/YIVqTjsebxoC?hl=en&gbpv=1&dq=Harry+Sinclair,+May+28,+1921++The+oil+weekly&pg=PA7556&printsec=frontcover.

Hofsommer, Donovan L. *Railroads in Oklahoma.* Oklahoma City: The Gateway to Oklahoma History, 1977.

Hoig, Stan. "Boomer Movement." http://www.okhistory.org/publications/enc/entry.php?entryname=BOOMER%20MOVEMENT.

———. "Land Run of 1889." http://www.okhistory.org/publications/enc/entry.php?entry=la014.

Indian Land Tenure Foundation. "History." https://iltf.org/land-issues/history/.

Jackson, R. J. "Deadly Affair: This Is the Tragic Story of a Man Who Seemingly Had It All; Jack Hammon's Connection to the Teapot Dome Scandal." *The Oklahoman.* http://newsok.com/article/3910896 (Link is dead.).

Kaye, Frances W. "Little Squatter on the Osage Diminished Reserve: Reading Laura Ingalls Wilder's Kansas Indians." *Great Plains Quarterly* 20.2 (May 2000) 123–40.

https://digitalcommons.unl.edu/cgi/viewcontent.cgi?referer=https://www.bing.com/&httpsredir=1&article=1022&context=greatplainsquarterly.

Lovegrove, Michael W. "Payne, David Lewis (1836–1884)." http://www.okhistory.org/publications/enc/entry.php?entry=PA028.

Malone v. Scott, OK 708 606 606 (Oklahoma Supreme Court 1916) (No. 158).

McCarthy, Robert. "The Bureau of Indian Affairs and the Federal Trust Obligation to American Indians." *BYU Journal of Public Law* 19.1 (2005) 4–160.

Miner, H. Craig. *The Corporation and the Indian: Tribal Sovereignty and Industrial Civilization in Indian Territory, 1865–1907*. Norman: University of Oklahoma Press, 1976.

Minor Indians in Oklahoma investigation [Congressional record]. (1914).

Mortgage of Real Estate of Nellie Fish, No. 9777, 1912 (County of Creek May 23, 1912).

Musslewhite, ynn., & Crawford, Suzanne Jones. "Barnard, Catherine Ann (1875–1930)." https://www.okhistory.org/publications/encyclopediaonline.

Oil and Gas Mining Lease of Nellie Fish, No. 10622, 1912 (County of Creek May 1, 1912).

Oklahoma Historical Society. "Springer Amendment." http://www.okhistory.org/publications/enc/entry.php?entry=SP016.

Oklahoma Historical Society Research Center, Archives of the Five Civilized Tribes, Ullie Eagle Files. June 23, 1913. Department of the Interior, Unites States Indian Superintendent, in the Matter of the Protest Against Approval of Oil and Gas Mining Liese #24200, Nellie Fish et al, as Sole Heirs of Ullie Eagle, Decese. Muskogee.

Orlowski, D. Faith, & Burke, Robbie Emery. "Oklahoma Indian Titles." *Tulsa Law Review* 29.2 (Winter 1993) 361–83.

O'Dell, Larry. "Clarke, Sidney (1831–1909)." http://www.okhistory.org/publications/enc/entry.php?entry=CL005.

Peters, G. &. W., J. T. (1879, April 26). "Rutherford B. Hayes Proclamation 243: Warning against unathorized settlement in the Indian Territory." https://www.presidency.ucsb.edu/documents/proclamation-243-warning-against-unauthorized-settlement-the-indian-territory.

———. (1885, March 13). "Grover Cleveland Proclamation 266: Prohibition of non-Indian settlement of Oklahoma lands in the Indian Territory." https://www.presidency.ucsb.edu/documents/proclamation-266-prohibition-non-indian-settlement-oklahoma-lands-the-indian-territory.

Posey, Alexander. (1906). A Memorial to the Congress of the United States on Behalf of the State of Sequoyah." https://babel.hathitrust.org/cgi/pt?id=loc.ark:/13960/t6qz2kf9k;view=2up;seq=6.

Prassel, Frank Richard. *The Western Peace Officer: A Legacy of Law and Order*. Norman: University of Oklahoma Press, 1972.

Prucha, Francis Paul. *Documents of United States Indian Policy*. Lincoln: University of Nebraska Press, 2000.

Reese, Linda W. "Women." https://www.okhistory.org/publications/enc/entry.php?entry=WO003.

Rice, G. William. "The Indian Reorganization Act—75 Years Later: Renewing Our Commitment to Restore Tribal Homelands and pPomote Self-Determination." https://www.indian.senate.gov/sites/default/files/upload/files/062311CHRG-112shrg68389.pdf.

Roosevelt, Theodore. "Do the People Rule in Oklahoma?" *The Outlook* 90.5 (October 3, 1908) https://babel.hathitrust.org/cgi/pt?id=msu.31293000744478&view=2up&seq=245&size=125&q1=do%20the%20people%20rule%20in%20oklahoma.

Rusco, Elmer R. *A Fateful Time: The Background and Legislative History of the Indian Reorganization Act.* Reno: University of Nevada Press, 2000.

Sahr, Robert. "Inflation Conversion Factors for Years 1774 to estimated 2028." https://liberalarts.oregonstate.edu/spp/polisci/research/inflation-conversion-factors.

State of Oklahoma, County of Tulsa, Petition in the Matter of Sarah Ann Perryman Kate Barnard - Commissioner of Charities and Corrections of the State of Oklahoma (County of Tulsa March 8, 1913).

Sutherland, J. J. "L. Frank Baum Advocated Extermination of Native Americans." *National Public Radio*, October 27, 2010. https://www.npr.org/sections/thetwo-way/2010/10/27/130862391/l-frank-baum-advocated-extermination-of-native-americans.

Tams Bixby investigation [Congressional record]. (1904). https://play.google.com/books/reader?id=D5zB-FIl3PwC&printsec=frontcover&output=reader&hl=en&pg=GBS.PA5318.

Tarbell, Ida M. *The History of the Standard Oil Company.* New York: McClure, Phillips, 1904.

Title 25-Indians CHAPTER 14-MISCELLANEOUS SUBCHAPTER V-PROTECTION OF INDIANS AND CONSERVATION OF RESOURCES 25 U.S.C United States Code (June 18, 1934).

Webster, Ian. "$1 in 1910 Is Worth $28.11 Today." Accessed on May 17, 2021. https://www.in2013dollars.com/us/inflation/1910?amount=1.

Williams, Geoff. "A Glimpse at Your Expenses 100 Years Ago." *U.S. News & World Report*, January 2, 2015. https://money.usnews.com/money/personal-finance/articles/2015/01/02/a-glimpse-at-your-expenses-100-years-ago.

Witgen, Michael. "A Nation of Settlers: The Early American Republic and the Colonization of the Northwest Territory." *The William and Mary Quarterly* 76.3 (July 2019) 391–98. https://www.jstor.org/stable/10.5309/willmaryquar.76.3.0391.

www.ingramcontent.com/pod-product-compliance
Lightning Source LLC
Chambersburg PA
CBHW070630310726
48982CB00001B/235

* 9 7 8 1 6 6 6 7 0 3 2 9 0 *